The Skin Factory

Lucas Pederson

LVP
PUBLICATIONS

Lycan Valley Press Publications
1625 E 72nd St STE 700 PMB 132
Tacoma, Washington 98404 United States of America

Printed in the United States of America

First Printing

ISBN-13: 978-1-64562-991-7

For my kiddos.
Always be you. Always shine.

INTRODUCTION

The idea for this book wouldn't have happened if not for my job assembling refrigerators for Whirlpool. If I was stuck on one job for the day (I was a plant utility and bounced around a lot), my mind would drift. Some ideas were just goofy, but then I happened to overhear a supervisor and co-worker joking around on the other side of the line. I can't remember all of conversation, but it kind of went down like this:

"Get back on the line," Mr. Supervisor said and chuckled.

I caught an exaggerated eyeroll by the co-worker through the small gaps of refrigerators. "Dude, you don't own me."

Mr. Supervisor clapped co-worker on the back and, in a lower voice said, "No, but I own your soul."

They both cracked up. Personally, I failed to see what was so funny. But that's okay because a new idea wormed it's way into my mind. Along with it came the question: What if evil beings stole human souls to build fake humans possessed by other evil entities to infiltrate Earth and gradually take over?

That's what started it all. In a couple months, the first draft was born.

So... thank you weird former supervisor and co-worker. Without you...this book might not have ever been thought of.

My children also played a large part in writing this book. They each gave me a sliver of their personalities. Mary, my oldest, gave me her warm hugs, passionate nature and the strongest hope. Hannah, the second oldest daughter, gave me strength and sarcasm. Emma, the youngest daughter, gave me inquisitiveness and laughter. Noah, the only boy, gave me heart and silliness.

Combined, they helped create the atmosphere of the book and the main character, Chase.

There's Mom, who never stopped believing in me and would listen to my book rants and woes with the sweetest bemused expression.

My mom passed away from ALS, and it's her courage, unstoppable will and compassion that I will carry forever.

I want to thank my love, Danielle. Without you, I wouldn't be who I am today. Thank you for your full support in everything I do.

Last, but not least, thank you, frantic reader. Us authors are always grateful for your love and love you in return.

Lucas Pederson
December 2019

OBSIDIOUS

~ 1 ~

Hᴇʟʟ? Sʜɪᴛ, ᴛʜᴀᴛ'ᴅ ʙᴇ like green grass and jellybeans compared to this.

There's a brutal *crack* and a whiff of hot bone as I jack the last of the cylindrical teeth into the upper jaw of the skull. I holster the Pop Gun and flex my iridescent hand from the heat of the thing. Using an angled mirror, I quickly inspect the teeth alignment. Details will be worked in later down the line in Final.

The teeth are perfect. No gaps.

I pat the skull containing the teeth I just installed, and the conveyor moves on.

A new unit arrives. Toothless, as they all are before they get to me. A jawless, empty skull tacked to a steel rack.

I re-draw the Pop Gun. It's still warm. As I grab a handful of unformed teeth from the yellow tote at my side , my gaze lifts to the clock attached to the I-beam on the other side of the line. Ten more minutes and I'm out of this shithole, thank the gods of purple jelly.

Rolling the teeth in my fingers, I load one into the business end of the Pop Gun. It makes a loud *psstuck* sound when the tooth enters the back socket. It'll be a molar once it's detailed.

Every day is the same. A stupid, endless cycle.

Beside me, Judith attaches the lower jaw. She does this without expression. She flickers sometimes, as a sign of depression. She dims when tired. As we all do. But she's been doing it a lot today. Might be nothing. I shoot her a smile and she returns it. Maybe she's okay, then? Hope so. She's been like a mother to me since I was plucked off my Path.

Everyone has an assigned job. Their place on the line. None of us have a choice.

The Factory is a place where human bodies are built for one purpose: to infiltrate humanity. Being empty shells, these units are easier to possess by cruel entities that call themselves Controllers. The possessed units are then transported to an adjacent world (my Earth) and the infiltration cycle continues. Thousands are transported daily. I dunno what the Wardens are planning, but it can't be good. At all. And the worst of it is… I can't stop them.

I'm on Line 1, which is Skull and Nervous System Assembly.

I pop in the remaining teeth, and the conveyor moves the skull to Judith. She attaches the lower jaw

—teeth pre-installed—and sends it on to Chuck, who pins the spine to the base of the unit.

Another unit stops in my station.

Guess I should consider myself lucky. At least I'm not stuck on Line 2-Skeletal Assembly. The line doesn't stop at all on that one. It keeps fucking going until the end of shift buzzer. No breaks, even.

Line 3, for installing hearts and organs, is faster yet.

Ten lines in all. The higher the number, the faster it moves.

Pop more teeth into a skull, send it on its way.

I'm about to start on the next when my sight catches the number engraved on the skull's forehead.

30-30-751

Shit. New model. 750s are bad, but the 751s—

"Number 51Z-60." A gentle voice floats from the factories speakers. "Your time limit is near. Install teeth or it's a week in the Hole."

Yeah, screw that. The Hole is the last place I want to be. There are... things down there. Things that nibble off tiny pieces of you for the duration of your stay. Some never make it out of the Hole.

I yank a red tote out from under the workbench and grab a handful of 751 teeth. The only difference I see is that they're smaller. They take no more than thirty seconds to pop in, but even that's too long.

The Wardens don't drag me away to the Hole,

though. Works for me.

Number 51Z-60? That's all I am to them. But I'm not a just a dumb number. I'm Chase Dunning. *Chase*, damn it. Not even this droning existence will suck that memory out of me.

The next 751 jerks to a stop in front of me.

Judith shoots me a concerned look. Probably wondering what stalled me for a couple seconds longer than usual. I shrug and keep working. We're not allowed to talk either. Which sucks.

My body brightens for an instant as a recurring thought ignites my mind. I try to dim it down so the Wardens' watchers don't see. I need to be careful; thinking of sabotaging the line always make me flare like that.

Force a shutdown, though, and we could all go to our cells for the day. We could rest.

Yes, even souls need rest.

Ticking away possible scenarios, I eventually abandon the idea. For now. Maybe later, though…

The Wardens are always watching. If they catch me messing with anything, I'll cease to exist. Or wish I had. Either way, they win. Our bosses aren't demons or devils, but creatures beyond all that. Things you never read about, but sometimes feel in the darkest of places. The chill crawling along your spine? Yeah, that's because of them. Not really sure what they are. And Aben, the Head Warden, is the worst.

Still, everything has a weakness. A flaw in the

system. It's just a matter of—

A deafening bray explodes through the factory. About friggin' time! Peace! Finally another shift of Factory hell behind me.

The conveyor stops. Second shifters step into the stations as we step out. Wordlessly.

Then we're herded out of the Factory—like damn cattle to the slaughterhouse—and into a massive building joined to it.

The Dwellings, the Wardens call it.

We call it Prison.

To say the least, we're all dim by the time they gather us in the Social Room. Which is just another name for Inspection Room.

They form us into single-file lines. We aren't allowed to talk during inspection.

The Stewards—hunched, pale things with bulging black eyes—test our levels, our auras, and our remembrance skills. Fail one test, and there are consequences. Fail two, they suck out some of your light. Fail all, and they extinguish you. Better that, though, than being tossed into the Hole. Bad things down there.

Someone nudges me. I gaze over my shoulder. It's Judith. Her aura flickers. Her light… dimmer than the others. Her white eyes have taken on a gray hue.

There's so much worry in her face it makes my own aura flicker. She's going to fail all the tests, and she knows it.

Shit.

Upon my arrival, Judith took me under her wing. She showed me the ropes, taught me the rules. And because of that I never received punishment. A fair share of warnings, but no punishments. No Rack (where your essence is stretched beyond its limits). No Hole.

I owe her my existence.

And she's going to fail the tests. They'll take her away and—

"Arms up, number 51Z-60." A Steward looms over me. Its bulging black eyes pulse in loose, pallid sockets. Its thin lips peel away from tiny, pointy teeth.

My essence chills. I hate these things. Scare the piss outta me. Well, if I *could* piss, that is. For all the time I've been here, I can't get past the utter creeps these monsters give me.

I lift my arms. The Steward places a giant claw on my chest. Its black eyes jitter wildly. Small sucking sounds fill my head.

"What is your job?" the Steward demands.

"Teeth installation. Line 1," I reply. Same shit every day.

"Do you know your name?"

"No," I lie. The Steward doesn't catch it. Never does.

"How long have you worked here?"

"I don't know." The truth. Time is weird here. Besides the work clocks, time seems irrelevant.

"How old are you?"

"Sixteen."

It's the age that sticks in my mind because that's when my body died.

"Join fellow workers in Common Area." The Steward removes its claw from my chest, motioning for me to move along.

I go to do just that, then pause. Glance over my shoulder at Judith.

"Join fellow workers in Common Area," the Steward repeats. To Judith it says, "Arms up, number 20B-80."

I begin walking away, hands clenched into fists.

Then Judith screams. A high-pitched shriek of pain.

I spin around just as the Steward rips the head from her body. Light sprays everywhere in a shower of sparks. Judith's severed head continues to scream.

"*No*," I cry, but the others (many of whom I call friends) hold me back from charging at the creature.

Judith's body crumples to the floor, flickers, goes dark. Vanishes. She's just been extinguished.

With a deep grunt, the Steward crushes Judith's screaming head between its massive claws. Sparks ignite the air and turn gray, like fallen ash, before disappearing.

I thrash against the hands holding me.

She's gone. *Gone*…

"You son of a *bitch!*"

The Steward turns to me. Its head cocks to the

side. "Number 51Z-60. Weren't you supposed to report to the Common Area as directed?"

A girl whispers in my ear, "Knock it off, Chase." Sara. Has to be. She connects the nerves to the spine further down the line. She's awesome. But right now I don't care who she is.

The bastards just killed the woman who pretty much saved me from going through inexplicable tortures.

"Number 51Z-60." The Steward approaches, head lowered. "Respond."

"You—" Someone kicks me. Hard. Probs Sara. It's enough to quell the boiling rage to a deep simmer. "Um, I mean, yeah. Common Area."

"And why are you not there?"

I try not glare when I speak. It's one of the hardest things I've ever had to do.

"She was a good friend."

It leans close, pointy teeth centimeters from my face. "We know." It straightens. "Last warning. Report to Common Area. Now."

The others turn me away from Judith's murderer. They release a collective sigh of relief through their beings I cannot share.

Some say souls can't cry. But by the time we reach the huge chain linked cage of the Common, it's all I can do.

~ 2 ~

GRAY FOG TWISTS AND SWIRLS.

When it clears, a slender hand holding a scalpel lowers the blade to the top of a small, furry head. A rat. Blood wells through grayish fur as the hand slips the blade lengthwise between pointy, pink ears.

The world shudders, and now a thumb and index finger hold open the furry scalp. A small marble is placed in the mess and the scalp stretched and stitched over it, creating a grotesque knob—

The fog billows in, obscuring everything.

A single name floats through the grayness in big red letters.

ANDI.

The fog evaporates, leaving me fully awake and lost.

Andi? My little sister, Andi? But why…

I'm awake, but not alone.

White eyes blink at me. A scream lodges in my throat. The stink gives my visitor's identity away, though. A thick, swampy stench.

"Word is," the thing looming over me says, "you were quite defiant today."

I sit up. "Bal?"

"Who else would be here so late? As your Counselor, I have to say I'm very disappointed in your behavior earlier."

Everyone is assigned a Counselor during the Taking. They're usually the ones who took you in the first place. Who ripped you off the Path to your destined After. They are the ones who watch over you and take care of you. Make sure you're burning bright and staying out of trouble. That's what they're supposed to do, I guess, but this is the first time I've seen Bal since my Taking.

It was Judith who really watched over me.

The Counselors also dole out punishments, everything from the Rack to the Hole. But they take their orders from the Wardens, as we all do.

Bal's white eyes narrow. "Care to explain yourself?"

"Um," I manage. "Judith was my friend. Sorry, I got mad. It wasn't right."

Bal stares at me for a long time. His smoky black body—tall and lean—shifts in and out of focus. Swirls. "You..." he says finally, "got mad? That's your excuse?"

"Well," I say. "Slaying a dragon was already

taken, so…"

"Funny. I see you're still as much a smartass as you were the moment I plucked you from the Path."

I grin. "You missed me."

Bal's eyes flash. "Careful, Chase. You'll turn a talk into a punishment."

So he's not here to hurt me. Well, hot diggity for that.

"You wanna… .talk?"

The Counselor moves closer, bends. "Yes. You're a first offender, and it's policy only to talk to you. One more, and your punishments begin. That, however, is up to you and what you take away from this little chat."

"Me? Dude, I can't punish myself. That'd be like —"

A cold, dark hand seizes my throat and squeezes. I'm beyond breathing, but his grip cuts off the light pulses to my mind. Things get all wavy. My light stutters. Okay. I get it.

"Foolish boy," Bal growls into my face. "You know what I mean." He releases me and backs away a bit. "Now, I'll make this brief. I know number 20B-80 was your friend. As I know that, because of her, you stayed out of trouble."

"Her name was Judith."

Bal waves a dark hand. "Names are irrelevant."

"You call me Chase."

White eyes flash again. "Because I am *your* Counselor."

I shrug, though keep quiet. Don't want to go overboard. Maybe it's Judith's voice in my head telling me to stop. Maybe not. All I know is it's better right now to just let it go.

"In any case," Bal continues. "Just because she was your friend does not give you the right to interfere with an extinguishing. And your disobedience has caught the attention of the Wardens. I need you to promise me you will never act like that again."

When I don't say anything, Bal sighs. The swampy stench suffocates the cell.

Thank the fake pink buffalos I don't have a gag reflex anymore or I'd be blowing chunks everywhere.

"Chase," Bal says. "I need your promise, and I need it now or the Wardens will toss you in the Hole for however long they see fit."

I knew a guy—Adam—who spent thirty working days in the Hole. He came back without a face and missing both hands. His aura was littered with hundreds of tiny, black bite marks.

Soul eaters dwell down there. The very thought sends a rill of pulsating light through me.

Bal notices this, straightens. "Chase? Are you ill?"

For a moment, all I can do is stare at him.

Saysomethingsaysomethingsaysomethingsay—

"I—no. Sorry. Yeah, I promise."

My Counselor falls silent for a long time. Like

he's on the verge of telling me something. Drives me fruitbatty when they go all dramatic pause on me like this. So… I break the quiet.

"We done?"

Bal sighs. "Yes. We are. Remember, they're watching you closely now. Any mistakes and not even I can stop them."

Not like you would anyway, I think. For some reason the thought strikes me as funny and a small laugh escapes my throat.

"I don't see what's so funny—"

"It's not," I say, swallowing more giggles down. "But I'm sure you're enjoying all this."

"Enjoying it… ? Chase, you are like my own son. More than you know. I don't enjoy any of this."

"*You* brought me here, asshat," I nearly shout. "If you really cared you would have let me continue on the Path and go to Heaven—"

The slap comes without warning. A loud *crack* that whips my head from side to side.

Bal growls into my face. "There is no *Heaven* for you. You would have been lost between worlds if not for me. Remember that." The creature leans closer to me, his stench overwhelming. "Keep your nose clean a little while longer, foolish boy." Then he turns away.

Okay? Whatever that means. "Hey, thanks for the talk," I say, rubbing my nonexistent cheek. "We made *so* much progress."

Bal doesn't speak again. He moves forward and

passes through the cell bars like black smoke. My Counselor vanishes, leaving me alone.

I lie down and try to rest. Souls don't really sleep, per se. More like going dormant. We blank out for awhile and call it rest. Our light is brighter when we get enough rest. We work better too. It's effin' crazy, but that's how it works.

Andi, I think.

She and I might be linked in some way. Are the dreams or visions really her? If not, who the demonsquirts is doing those bod-mods on animals? This is like the hundredth vision/dream I've had of someone cutting into an animal, or tattooing pink skin, or… whatever. I hope it's not Andi. Not my goofy, artistic sister. As far as I knew, she never dabbled in the bod-mod thing.

The thought of her spurs another jolt through me. Possessed units are mingling with humans for dark purposes, and she's out there. Mom too. Dad has to be in prison for what he did. Killing your own son isn't exactly smiled upon by many. The douchenozzle.

I listen to the ticking of the huge clock near the Guard booth below me. The faster the ticking, the closer it is to work time. Judging by the slow, spaced out ticks, I have a while.

Maybe long enough to check something out.

I leave my cell.

All the lines run on the Central Motor, which feeds power to the smaller motors throughout the Factory. Take out Central, and the rest will follow. Problem is, that's damn near impossible.

The Central Motor is in the basement of the Factory. In order to get near it, you either need to be assigned to work down there, or be someone of importance. Like a Steward, I guess.

Anyone else caught in the basement is extinguished on the spot. No Hole. No second chances. Just, *poof*, gone.

So, me being down here now instead of resting in my cell is pretty effin' fruitbatty. There are eyes everywhere, but so far no alarms sound.

Keeping to the dark sides of a damp hall that seems to have been decorated in nothing but rusted metal, I force my light to dim as much as possible without making me pass out. Sucks, but needs to be done if I don't want to get caught.

A loud *KA-Chung-KA-Chung*, vibrates the floor beneath me. The sound of some heavy-ass machinery, for sure. I must be getting close.

A waning light ahead marks my destination. Or at least I hope so. Don't want to be wandering around down here longer than I need to. If the light isn't Central, I'll have to return to my cell and try again tomorrow night. Fruitbatty or not, this needs to be done if I even want a minimal chance of escaping.

Few more yards, and voices filter through the

*KA-Chung*s. They speak in a chirping bird language. That's if your birds have deep, growling voices, anyway. Which is absurd. Quick, throaty chirps.

The light ahead flickers, strengthens, dims, brightens.

I venture on. The closer I get to the light and voices, the more I realize there must be a huge chamber or room ahead. The way the voices echo off the stone walls is a dead giveaway. Then again, nothing is always what it seems in this wretched place.

I arrive at a sharp corner and stop. Yep. A massive room. The corridor gives way to it. Across the room is a tall, black archway. But there's no sign of the Central Motor, nor the sources of the voices. Unless...

Peer around the corner and—

A hand slaps onto my shoulder. I almost scream.

Then a whisper, "Shh. It's me."

Sara smiles when I turn. Her light is also dim. There's worry roiling in her eyes, though. Gray squiggles in all the white.

"What are you doing here?" I whisper.

She plants her hands on her hips, cocks her head to the side. Pretty much asking me the same question in gesture.

I shrug. She rolls her eyes.

Man, I wish I would've met her in life. I bet she was—

Sara yanks me away from the corner, slams me

into the stone wall. My mouth opens to give her shit about it and she shakes her head, points at the opposite wall of the corridor.

Two hulking shadows consume the other wall. They swell all the way to ceiling.

My light waxes and wanes. Sputters. Dammit. Stop being fruitbatty, light. Stop it right now or no rest for you!

I'm an idiot.

Thick-soled boots scuff the stone floor. Their deep bird voices move closer.

Press my back flat against the wall. The chill I feel isn't the stone, but my own terror. If they see Sara or me, that'll be the end. Not a single spark of us left when they get through.

The first one rounds the corner. It's a giant. Larger than the Stewards. This monster towers over us by at least four feet. The breadth of its shoulders nearly touch both walls of the corridor.

Guards. The Factory's security. Hot-headed beasts. If it notices us—

It glances over its immense shoulder, gibbers something, laughs. An enormous rumbling laughter that quakes my aura.

Directly behind the first Guard is another. They're both dressed in all blue denim. Or at least it looks like denim. Similar to bib-overalls, I guess.

I think, *Bubba.*

I think, *Ah, shit, it's the Bubba Twins.*

Giggles bubble up my throat. I swallow them

down quickly. Sara's hand finds mine, squeezes tight. I squeeze back.

The second Guard (Bubba #2), shakes its large head, shoves Bubba #1. Bubba #1 stumbles, laughs.

Bubba #2 only grunts. I don't like that one. It's too watchful. Its green eyes continually shift. The nostrils of its ape-like face flare, taking in quick snorts of air. Searching for an odd sent. If it smells us...

They lumber by without pause and before long disappear up the corridor.

Relief floods over me, changing my pulsating light to a deep blue. Cheese'n'rice, that was close.

When we can't hear their gibbering anymore, Sara punches my arm. Hard. It doesn't hurt, but—

"Hey," I say. "What was that—"

"What the hell are you doing down here," she growls.

"Looking for something. What are you doing?"

"I saw you sneak by my cell, dumbfrits. Made me curious Looking for what?"

"Oh, nothing important." I wave a hand. "Go back. I'll see you at work."

"I'm not going anywhere," Sara says. "Tell me what you're doing."

I grab her shoulders. "Look. If you're caught you'll be—"

Sara yanks out of my grip. "Put in the Hole? Yeah, so will you. That's if they don't just extinguish your ass, which they probably will."

"Yeah… they will." I glance around the corner and smile. There it is. What I risked my existence for.

The Central Motor isn't what I expected, though. I envisioned a large, shiny engine with pistons and gears and belts, supplying power to the Factory through thick wires.

But the thing around the corner is a monstrosity that more resembles a giant pot-belly stove than any motor I've ever seen. Huge, rusty tubes snake from the top of it in all directions, disappearing into the stone ceiling. Purple fire roils behind a blackened grate.

KA-Chung, KA-Chung, KA-Chung.

As steady as, well, a heartbeat.

There's no question in my mind that this beastly thing is the Factory's heart. It pumps power into the place. Not only the smaller motors, but the lights, *everything.* Stop the Central Motor, and the Factory dies.

Surrounding the motor are massive mounds of amber colored stones. Not coal… but these… whatever they are. Never saw anything like them, so it's hard to say.

KA-Chung, KA-Chung, KA—

"*Chase.*" Sara swings me back to her. "We have to go. Someone's coming."

I frown. "Someone—"

Then I hear them. Voices bouncing off the stone walls. Not the throaty chirps of the Guards, but the stilted speech of Utilities. Beings that are fill-ins on the line if labor is short. They clean up messes, and—

Six of them emerge from the dark archway across the room, snatching up scoop shovels on their way to the Central Motor. They're naked, save for twists of tattered cloth around their loins. Their skin isn't skin at all, but tiny gray scales. Faces that'll give any kid nightmares for months. Slack-jawed, toothy maws snap sporadically. Wide, opaque eyes roll in constant vigilance. Their faces remind me of those deep sea fish. The ones that lure their prey by dangling a bulb of organic light fixed on their head. The ones with long, sharp teeth.

"Can'believe," One shouts over the noise of the motor. "We takin' business from humans again."

They open the giant grate and purple fire whooshes outward. None of them appear too concerned by this. The fire sucks back into the opening.

They shovel the amber stones into the fire. It flares, roars and hisses with every scoop. Brightens so much it blinds me for a few seconds.

If I'd been looking through the eyes of my human body, my retinas would've surely been burned.

"Ah," another Utility shouts. "Been doin' dat f'long while. Ya know dat. I hear dat girl'es good wit skin changin' anyhow."

"We make our own skin," cries yet another.

"Doh's units don'need special skin."

One nearest to Central shrugs. "She fail soon. You see. Dey all do."

They fall silent for a little bit, shoveling amber stones. Feeding the unearthly fire.

I have no idea what they're talking about. Skin? It's true, we manufacture our own skin for the units. Simple process actually. And who is this girl they're talking about? Is someone supplying real skin? How? And why?

"Aben a fool," pipes the one to the right of the motor.

"Nah," says another. "He smart."

Aben. Everyone knows that name. The Head Warden. The Grand Poo-Bah. The bastard in charge. Saw him once, and could barely look at him. Not because he's ugly or anything. No. He's like some flawless model in an ad for Armani or something. So perfect in every way, it gave me the chills by just the sight of him.

"Aben'll meet girl person'ly, I get," one Utility pipes.

"Yar," another says and tosses a scoopful of amber stones into the fire.

Whoosh.

"Him'n Ti."

"Ti love me," one Utility I can't see says.

This is followed by howling laughter. When it dies down, the one closest to the motor shouts, "Ya wish."

Two at a time, they shovel stones into the fire.

Ti is Aben's liaison. His assistant. Second in command. Pretty, with a coldness that seems deeper than her boss. Talk about scary? The chick will rip the Source right out of you all while painting her long fingernails and whistling "I'm a Little Tea-Pot."

I won't be doing any damage to the Central Motor tonight. No way I can get past the Utilities without being spotted. Maybe tomorrow—

Sara tugs on my arm.

Yeah. Time to go. At least I know there's a slim possibility of doing some damage. The Utilities go on break and the Guards keep watch. Guards leave; Utilities return. The scattering of seconds between this change is my window. It's not much, but it's the best chance.

We're turning to leave when a Utility says, "Can't wait till dey let dat Obsidious loose on h'umans. Won't have'ta worry 'bout dem den."

I stop, pull Sara back. My head cocks to the side, trying to hear the creatures better. Sara growls, yanks on my arm. I shake my head and hold up a silencing hand. She rolls her eyes.

"I hear dat brudder. Obsidious will take care of dem."

"Obsidious," I whisper.

Sara slaps a hand over her face. A dramatic face-palm. She grabs my shoulders and begins leading me away again.

"Yup," a Utility says. "End'em all, I say. Not'in

but pests an'how."

"Da Obsidious'll eat away da pestiest parts."

It's the last thing I hear before Sara drags me far enough away that their voices become nothing but garbled mumbling drowning in the constant *KA-Chungs* of the Motor.

She doesn't have to drag me for long. Soon we're running to the vent I snuck through to get down here.

I think, *The Guards will be waiting*.

I think, *We're so screwed*.

But there are no Guards in sight and the vent grate appears as I left it: slightly askew for quick access. We shrink, and dive through the small gap and into the rust flecked duct beyond. Shrinking is the worst energy suck ever. A few feet in, I need to stop and rest a bit. My light fades in and out. A soul's version of being winded.

Spent *way* too much time in the bowels of the Factory.

"Chase, for shit sake, *c'mon*." Sara tugs on me to move.

My light still fades in and out, but not as badly.

We keep moving.

Up and up, scaling the old duct with what little energy we still possess. We're on the Main Floor of the Factory in no more than a minute. I secure the upper grate on the vent and scan the crumbling bathroom around us. Souls don't poop or pee, so I don't know why a bathroom was built in the first place. Maybe that explains the crumbliness of it. I dunno.

All around us, the Factory thrums. An unrelenting beast.

Now comes the tricky part. Sneaking to the Prison and past the Guard Booth in the Social Room—aka, the Inspection Room—to Cell Block A. There are eight Guards in and around the booth. All older, seasoned creatures. Always vigilant and quick to act.

The Wardens constantly monitor the Factory, but there are plenty of shadows for us to use and it takes no time at all until we emerge in the hall between Factory and the Prison.

We slip out of the shadows and speed low to the floor all the way to the Guard Booth. Throaty chirps filter through the thin walls of the booth. Language of the Guards, but there is also a smattering of English in there too.

One sentence rises above the babbling.

"We'll be outta jobs when they release the Obsidious."

Obsidious again. Have the Guards and Utilities been talking about this for long? Or is it something new? I never really paid much attention to what they talk about before. Maybe I should have. Wow.

I still have no clue what Obsidious is, but it sounds bad. Like some horrible plague. The way the Utilities talk about it, maybe I'm not so far off in this assumption. Something to hurt human souls.

Which means my mom and Andi are in danger.

Sara rushes to her cell.

I pass through the bars of my own.

We made it back safe. But this does little to quell the throbbing terror coursing through me. Not only for myself, but for Sara now too.

She risked a lot following me tonight. And I think I've fallen in love with her a little bit more because of it.

Whatever the Obsidious is, it puts Mom and Andi in even more danger. Yeah, time to figure out a way out of this shithole. The Docks are the only way. If I can figure out how to get through them, though...

I lie on my cot and drift into the gray fogs...

"Thief!" A loud crow-like squawk explodes through the gray. Sight shifts to a small bag of dog food clutched in the crook of an arm.

Stole something. On the run. Cops coming. Gotta hide under a residential porch or...

The fog shimmers, blots out the world and suddenly there stands a bronze-skinned girl on a cement patio. Staring at her phone. Texting. Maybe. And—

Fog billows, clears, and the bronze-skinned girl is closer. She says, "I'm Harper."

But that's not her name. It's... it's...

She continues, "And you are?"

A pause, then... "Andi."

Gray films over the vision, slips away.

In a bowl is a heap of what looks like homemade mac and cheese. The girl that is Not Harper says, "I have a friend who can help you get your own bod-mod shop."

Blink. The mac and cheese squirms with thin black worms.

Blink. Not Harper says, "His name is Aben and he looks like a model. I'll have him meet you."

"Okay."

The Wake Up buzzer snaps the gray fog out of me.

I sit, drained, dim, and beyond scared.

~ 3 ~

KEEPING MY LIGHT bright throughout the morning is a task unto itself.

By lunch, the dimming becomes noticeable.

"You okay?" Sara asks from across the table where we always sit. Closest to the vending machines.

"Do I *look* okay?"

Her eyes lower a bit. "No."

Neither does she. Her light is dimmer than mine. Fades with every passing minute. Not good. *So* not good.

I hold her hand gently in mine. "Sorry. Just grouchy."

"I know," she says. "It's okay, hun."

We're quiet for a while. The others in the Break Room talk amongst themselves. Rolling hills of voices.

Chuck sits beside me, grimacing at the gray

goop on the blue tray in front of him. Stuff that looks like a mound of very old oatmeal. Soul Meal, they call it. Ha-ha, joke's on us. Supposed to give us sustainable energy for the rest of the day. It does, but looks gross and thankfully we can't really taste it. Not in the literal sense anyway.

Chuck shifts his gaze from me to Sara. "You two did somethin', didn't ya." Not a question.

Jumping baby hippos, is it that obvious?

When we don't respond, he shoots us mild glances. "What? It's clear as day. Your auras are all wavy and your lights are dim."

"We—" Sara begins, but Chuck lifts a silencing hand.

"I don't need to know what, girly. What I'm gettin' at, though, is if *I* can see it, so can *they*."

I knew this already, but having Chuck point it out is like a hard slug to the gut.

"If I were you two," Chuck continues, pokes at the mound of goop on his tray. "I'd eat as much of this crap as possible before the buzzer."

Chuck slides the tray to Sara. She frowns at the Soul Meal, shakes her head and pushes it back.

"Not hungry," she says.

Chuck rolls his eyes and shoves the tray back. "Don't care if ya are or not. Eat it. If you wanna see tomorrow, eat it right now, girly." His gaze levels on me. "Better get yourself a tray too, son."

He's right. Sara and I eat the gray slop.

The energy lasts all day, even when we return to

our cells after work. Even as I sneak out of my cell in the dead of night all super ninja so Sara stays put.

I slip into the vent and follow the duct to the basement.

Tonight is the night. If I don't get out I'll be extinguished in no time. I need to find Andi and Mom before it's too late.

And the Obsidious?

One thing at a time, dammit.

The corridor is empty when I emerge from the vent, thank the gods and crunchy peanut butter. I wait to make sure Sara isn't following me this time. If she is she's hiding in the duct. Hopefully she stays in her cell tonight. Never forgive myself if she's punished because of my stupidity.

The *KA-Chung, KA-Chung* of the Central Motor trembles my being as I approach the huge room. The throaty chirps of the Guards filter through.

Timing will mean everything tonight.

Ten feet from the corner there's a shallow alcove. I duck into this and dim my light. Now… the wait.

The Guards lumber by without pause.

I count in my head.

One.

Two.

Three.

Four.

Five.

Six.

They're about twenty yards away now. Their deep chirps, barely echoes.

Seven.

Eigh—

Eff it. Close enough.

I dart out of the alcove and round the corner into the Motor Room. Sprint to the Motor. A weird heat blasts into me from the roiling purple fire. A heat that doesn't burn. Tiny needles pricking me, is what it feels like. More irritating than painful.

The Motor is immense and—sweet Judas, where's the fruitbatty OFF switch?

I'm hurrying around the fat belly of the beast when the skewed voices of the Utilities sound. But the archway is still dark and the room still empty, save for me. So far, at least.

Go.

In the very back of the Motor there's not a switch, but something just as good. A control panel set in the stone wall and wired to the Motor with thick cables.

It's so damn loud back here I can't hear if the Utilities are in the room. They're probably here, though. Already have their shovels, getting ready to bitch about random crap as they feed the Motor its amber fuel.

I scan over the panel. Buttons everywhere.

Of course, simply pushing a button won't shut the Factory down for long. It needs to be something more... substantial. Something permanent. Or at least long enough to distract the Wardens so I can escape. The Docks are my only option of getting out of this skewed world. Only problem with that plan is: Souls can't transport through the Docks on their own.

I need to break the Central Motor. Somehow...

Easier said than done. The thing is ginormous.

My sight glides over the cables connecting the panel to the Motor. These are my best bet, and easiest to fix, probably. If I cut or pull them, the Mechanics will no doubt have the lines up and running by the time my shift starts.

No, dammit. I need something...

My gaze happens on an old shovel with a bent handle a couple feet to the left of the control panel. Must've been back here for quite some time, judging by all the rust caking it. A castaway tool.

It's perfect.

I pick up the old, bent thing and look at the control panel.

A grin spreads along my face.

"Let's break shit," I whisper and swing the shovel.

The edge slams into the panel. Sparks erupt in a sparkling fount. A series of loud pops, like gunshots, blast through the air.

I yank the shovel free and strike the panel again, and again.

A deafening *bang* sounds a second before all the

lights go out and I'm doused in darkness.

White sparks spray from the panel, cascade to the floor.

Beside me, the Central Motor loses its shit. Sparks fly in every direction. The thunderous *KA-Chung*'s stop. Something inside the huge pot-belly shrieks. Green emergency lights flicker on.

"Ah, wad'ta *hell*," cries a Utility.

"What happen?" Another shouts.

"Som'thin wit da Motor. Call Sherm."

Sherm is the Factory's top Mechanic. He's also a grotesque asshole. Fat and mean.

"Som'thin wrong wit da panel," a Utility says.

"Hol'on. Gotta shut Motor down or it'll 'splode."

There's a sharp clicking noise then the Central Motor's gears whir down until the only sounds are of the fire inside the pot-belly and the Utilities.

"See'em sparks shootin'? Ah, happy-crap, tis busted *bad*."

Heavy footfalls thud closer, scratch to a halt. One of them is very close.

I quickly back away from the sputtering panel.

"Ya call Sherm?"

"Yar. He comin'. Why it sparkin' like dat?"

Electric snaps the air. A shower of sparks pour onto the floor.

I jog around the motor and sprint across the expanse of the room, dodging mounds of amber stones, and keeping as low to the ground as possible. The corridor isn't far. I can make it. I round a huge mound of stones and shoot for the corridor.

"*Hey*, look'it," a Utility shrieks. "Isn't dat a—"

"Get it," another roars.

Ah, hell.

Heavy boots clomp, echoing through the room, matching the intense fluttering of my light.

Chills pulse at my center. My feet make no sound against the stone floor of the gloomy corridor. We don't have enough mass to produce such noises.

The vent is only a few feet ahead. I charge full speed towards it. Time to go.

"It gettin'way," a Utility shouts.

"We got'im," another shouts back.

And holy poop stains, they're *gaining*.

Doesn't matter. I leap through the gap in the vent and scramble up the duct. A series of wails and curses blast at me from below. As fast as the bastards are, they can't shrink themselves like we can.

My entire being is like a large strobe light. Flashing like friggin' crazy. Okay, maybe I need a bit of a rest before going on. If I step out now I'll be like a damn beacon. Might as well have a huge neon sign with an arrow pointing at my head reading: HERE HE IS!

I need—

A huge, pale claw slams through the vent grate. Metal shrieks as it's sheared away. Gray talons slash, whickering centimeters from my face.

Holy *poopnuggets*! I recede further into the duct.

Away from the clutching, slashing claw and its wicked talons.

This isn't a Guard. Their skin is a blotchy peach color. Not a Steward either, with their leathery brown epidermis.

So... what the—

Low chuckling drifts through the duct. The pale claw vanishes.

The chuckling quickens my center's pulse. My light goes nuts. Blinks wildly. It's too dim to strobe now, I guess.

"Ah," speaks a whispering voice. "Chase. Here you are. Took me a while to figure out what you were up to, but no matter."

That voice. I know it, somehow.

"Might as well come out and join us, fearless child."

The word "child" ignites a searing heat through me. Pisses me off. I'm not a friggin' child!

"Come on, Chase." My name reverberates around me like dozens of ping-pong balls bouncing off the rusty surface of the duct. "You can't stay in there forever."

"Oh," I say. "I'm pretty sure I can."

A pause. "In two minutes," whispers the familiar voice, "Worms will be released into the duct. Do you know what these creatures will do to you?"

I don't. Probably something horrible. But, the owner of the whisper might be lying. Trying to scare me out like a rabbit from its hole. The Worms are just smoke.

"Shall I educate you, Chase? Worms, my boy, are unique creatures. Very old. Perhaps older than Earth's sun. And they do one thing above all else. They eat. But not before they burrow into their hosts and chew out all sanity."

Sharp screeching from the other end of the duct. The vent grate being torn off? I think so.

"I suggest you come out right now, Chase. Besides, you don't want to keep us waiting too long, now would you? Say hello, my sweet."

A scream slams into me hard enough to drive me back a few inches. Pain and terror, this is what it stabs me with. High and loud.

"Shh," whispers the voice and gradually the scream ends. "There, now. Why don't you tell him —"

"*Chase*," Sara cries. "Don't come out! It's a lie! Don't—"

The last is cut off by another shrill scream.

"Sara? *Sara*?" I start towards the ruined vent. "Stop hurting her you asshole—"

The pale claw rams through the opening. Its talons sink into my forearm. Pain—only vaguely reminiscent of the time my dad stabbed me in the arm with a fork for taking another helping of meatloaf—explodes. I cry out, try to pull away. There's nowhere to go. They have me and they mean to destroy me.

Something icy licks the side of my face. A light

chittering noise drifts through the duct. Oh, crap, is it a Worm?

There's no time to find out. The claw yanks me out of the duct before comprehension takes hold. Probably for the best, anyway. Or maybe not.

The claw opens and I drop to the floor. I scramble to my feet, about to run.

"No, Chase," a gentle voice said. "Don't run." Gentle in tone it might be, but underneath there's snake-like undertones. If I run, I'll be extinguished for sure.

The thing towering over me is tall, gangly, its skin the color of curdled milk. Its eyes are thin, green slits cut into an elongated face. Long, pointy teeth spout from a massive maw in skewed directions.

A low growl rumbles.

"This," says the gentle voice, as a man rounds the creature and places a well manicured hand on the monster's ropey arm, "Is an Ik."

The man flashes a set of brilliantly white teeth at me. A perfect smile. He's average height, dressed in an all white suit. His skin is smooth, tan, flawless. Bright, blue eyes hold my sight.

"Long ago," says the man—who most certainly isn't a man—as he moves towards me, "these were considered the highest quality of security. Protectors. Bred to serve and destroy. In a time well forgotten, they watched over kings, and yes, even devils." The man flicked a hand. "Ah, but then came the Reckoning. The war and movements within this world. Nearly every Ik was destroyed. I managed to save a few from extinction. They truly are magnificent creatures."

"Who are you?" I ask.

The man grins. "We've met before, Chase. I looked different then. My structure shifts year to year."

"I don't—"

"Ah, but you *do*. Think, boy."

It takes a handful of seconds. A chill spikes through my center.

"Aben," I whisper.

"Bravo." The Head Warden claps his hands together. I jump.

Last time Aben showed himself, it was because of a small mutiny. Sixty souls stepped off the line. They were all extinguished, one by one in front of us… by Aben. He smiled while he ate them. It was sick as hell.

"So," Aben says now, clasping his hands behind his back and moving closer. "What should we do about your little antics lately, hmm?"

Have to keep your cool, man, I think.

"Up yours, assface," I spout.

Face-palm.

Quickly I add, "Where's Sara?"

Aben blinks. For a while, all he does is stare at me. The smug grin never leaves his face.

Then, "*Chase.*" Sara's voice blasts out of Aben's

mouth. "Don't come out! It's a lie!" The Head Warden's lower jaw unhinges and a shrill scream pummels into me.

The scream fades as Aben closes his mouth. Deep chuckles follow.

"You pretended to be her," I shout, voice trembling. "You… you friggin' *tricked* me!"

Aben laughs, pats my shoulder. "Yes, my boy. I knew if anything would get you out—"

"And the Worms were a lie too?"

Aben's smile droops a bit. "Oh. No. Those are very real." He points at the ruined vent. "They're in there right now. Take a look, if you wish."

I glance over my shoulder. "Yeah, I'll pass."

"I bet you're wondering why I haven't extinguished you yet?" Aben asks.

"Crossed my mind," I reply. The Ik's nasty breath buffets my aura. A putrid dead-fish stink.

Aben nods. "Yes. I'm sure. You see, I admire your courage. Your will to seek answers no matter the consequences. To try and stop the Factory from running. Which you succeeded in, by the way. Bravo. This is why I haven't ordered my Ik to extinguish you, and why I haven't done so myself."

Okay… that doesn't seem like a very good reason.

"I want you to be my Scout, Chase."

Blink. "Huh?"

Aben's grin lengthens. "My Scout. Consider it a promotion."

I'm curious, despite the nagging pull from within to run as fast and far as I can away from this fiend.

"Uh, okay, so what's a Scout?" I ask.

But the Head Warden shakes his head. "Not here. Too many prying ears. Let's go to my office and—"

Aben's head tilts to one side. His blue eyes squirm with black squiggles. His upper lip curls in something between a sneer and a smile. It's a good minute or two before he straightens, adjusts the lapels of his white suit, and clears his throat.

"Seems, there's a matter," Aben says, "that requires my immediate attention." He turns and begins walking away, Ik in tow.

"So what do I do now?" I call after him.

Aben doesn't even look back when he replies. "I'll send a Guard to escort you to your cell. In the morning, we'll talk."

Then Aben and the Ik wink out of sight, leaving me completely alone in the men's room.

At least for now. Aben's Guard will be coming soon.

Anyway... a Scout? A promotion for breaking pretty much every rule, and then some? And, why do I care? I can still run. Right now. The Docks are always open. Even if I can't—

The door to the bathroom creaks open and a deep voice says, "Here to escort you to Cell C13. You have six seconds to respond."

Well, running is out.

I walk to the door. "Ready, asshat."

On our way to my cell, I can't help but wonder if this is all some elaborate trick. Soften me up.

The Guard opens my cell, gestures for me to enter.

I do. I feel the Guard's hatred pulsing into me in small, hot blasts.

Still, I grin and wiggle my fingers at it as I step into my cell.

The door slams shut behind me.

The Guard is walking away by the time I turn around, its heavy plods trembling the narrow catwalk. Soon I find myself lying on my cot, rapt in thought.

Then the creature looming over me says, "So… he gave you a promotion."

It's too late. I have just enough time to sit up before cold, black claws wrap around my throat. The world fogs over and returns in gray waves. Crashing, trying to push and pull me at the same time like a massive tide.

When I can sit up, and spare a few glances around, I find I'm in some steel-lined room. A vault of some sort. The only thing not shiny is the creature standing over me. Its white eyes convey indifference, though its voice…

"I am sorry, Chase," Bal says. There's genuine gentleness in the tone. "Didn't mean to knock you out so hard."

Shake my head and stand. "Yeah, well, a little warning next time would be nice. What's going on?"

Bal nods his dark head. Even the bright fluorescent lights above can't penetrate such darkness. "There's something you need to know before accepting the promotion, Chase. Something vital."

"What, for shit sake? Dude, why you gotta be so damn vague?"

Bal waves a black claw. "Smartass," he grumbles. "If you decline Aben's offer, he'll extinguish you and your girlfriend. And a few others to prove a point."

"Sara? Why her? She didn't—"

"She's close to you. He'll extinguish her and anyone else you've been seen with over the past couple weeks."

That means Chuck too. That's messed up. Chuck's just a kind old man.

"What I'm saying is," Bal continues, "you have two clear choices, and one gray one. Accept Aben's offer and become his Scout—his slave in other words. Or you decline and he extinguishes you and all your friends."

"And… the gray?"

Bal lowers his black, smoky head. When he looks at me his white eyes are blazing. "Run. Escape to your world and disappear."

"Disappear," I whisper. Then it dawns on me. "Why are you helping me? What's in it for you?"

"Chase, there's no time for—"

"No, dammit. Why? You steal me from my After, put me in this nasty place, and now out of nowhere you want to help me escape? Dude, you make no sense."

Bal's white eyes shift to a silver door to my right, lower. He faces me. "You remind me a lot of my son."

"I-wait, what? *You* have a *son*?"

The smoky creature nods. "Had. Long since has he been in his After. His body died centuries ago."

For a few moments, I'm speechless. Because, *what*? Then, "So… like you used to be human?"

"We really don't have time for this right now, foolish boy."

"Man," I say. "I'm just trying to understand. If you want me to trust you…" I let it hang there between us.

Bal swishes his smokiness away. He whispers, "Why am I helping you now? After all this time? I took you off your Path because you reminded me of my son, Saul, yes. Which is also one reason why I'm helping you now. The other reason is because I finally set things into motion for a rebellion, of sorts. To stop Aben from what he's doing. Set things right."

"That's all really cool and all, but why help me escape? Just because I remind you of your son?

Bal faces me again. "And you deserve to be with your family. In a few hours my legion will destroy the Factory and everything in it."

Blink. "But what about—"

"The souls will be set free to their Afters. Do not worry."

"Oh." I want to ask about Sara. If maybe she can come with me but…

I glance around. "Where am I?"

"A room between rooms. A place neither in the Factory, nor out of it."

Yeah, like that makes sense. "Sorry I asked. And how am I going to escape?"

Without pause, "The Docks. It's the only way out of here."

"The Docks," I whisper, remembering my own thoughts of escape. It's true. The Docks are the only way out. But… "Souls can't travel through the Docks. Only solid matter can—what? Why are you looking at me like that?"

A gray line lifts on Bal's dark face. *That's* his smile? Yikes.

"You'll see," he says and turns to the silver door. "Follow me. Don't hesitate when you step through."

He opens the silver door and moves through the opening.

"Hey, sure," I spout. "Thanks for the tip, jackass."

Still, I follow. And, of course I hesitate halfway through the doorway. Why do I have to think so much before acting? Because I'm a dumbass, that's why. A dumbass who—

We're standing near the Docks. The doorway

must've been a portal of some kind.

The alarms slam into my being with every shrill, *REEEE-REEEE-REEEE*.

"Foolish boy," Bal snaps, and yanks at me. I stumble forward.

Ahead the Docks are wavering, black rectangles cut into the very fabric of existence. Might as well call them portals, or riffs. Human units stand ramrod straight, single file, in front of each dock. Hundreds ready to deploy. They're strapped to narrow sheets of wood, which will be removed before loading. They're ready for transport. All they need are entities to—

Harried shouts leak through the constant shrillness of the alarms. Throaty chirps.

Guards, though I don't see them anywhere. Still, judging by their shouts, they're close.

Bal shoves me. Hard. "*Go.*"

I climb onto the line—still shut down because of me—and start towards Dock 1.

I stop, turn to Bal. He slaps a black claw to his forehead, as if to say, "Duh," and points at the unit beside me.

A boy—close to the age I was before Dad got a little too drunk one night and slammed a fist into my temple. His face has been modified some by implants, tattoos and piercings. I like him instantly. The only thing untouched is the hair. Which is dark blond, messy, and limp.

"Stop stalling and get in," Bal says. He looks at

me from the floor, white eyes wide.

Blink. "Uh, I don't know how to possess units, man. How—"

"There," the deep chirping voice of a Guard sounds. "On the line! Dock 1! All commence! He's on Dock 1!"

"Pay no attention," Bal says, pulling me out of a terror-stricken daze. "They're still a ways off. Their sight is stronger than yours." He points at the boy unit. "Get in. It's now or never."

"I said I don't know how to—"

"Go in through the ear. Get to the brain. Not hard. Once you're in it'll all come back to you. Just *go*."

"Dock 1! Seize'n'capture!"

My light flickers with panic. I pick out several large forms hurtling this way down the aisle. They'll be here soon. Too soon, maybe.

"Chase," Bal says. "Listen to me. Get in the unit. I promise everything will be okay."

Without thinking, I spin around and dive into an ear-hole.

From the outside, Bal shouts, "*No*. You idiot!"

Well, what the hell? Jeez. He's the one who…

Sporadic flashes assault my sight as I flail into the unit's brain. Crazy noises explode around me. Groans. Squeaks. Chutterings. The flashes stop and darkness swells in, leaving only the eerie sounds for company.

Floating, a sharp pain zaps through me like an

electrical shock. I jitter. A scream rips out of me and is immediately swallowed by a tremendous series of booms. Cannon fire are what these sound like. Deep. Shaky. Loud.

Good god, what's happening here? Do the Controllers feel this when they possess a unit? If so, they're insane to even accept the job. This is so not cool. I have to get out before something—

All the noises dull to a low roar. A loud *snick* echoes through the unit's brain. Lights set in short, red walls burst to life, obliterating the thick darkness. They're round, these lights. Might as well be dozens of glaring eyeballs.

Somewhere an odd humming noise rises and falls.

It takes me a while to realize that the deep *fa-thud-fa-thud-fa-thud* is the unit's heart.

There's an underwater bubbling of what might be voices. I'm not sure. More like groans. They rise and fall, echo through the weird room I'm stuck in.

All the lights flicker off and I'm submerged in complete darkness again. Really? Getting kind of sick being trapped in the dark all the time. Ever since I arrived to the Factory, it's been off and on darkness for me. Sucks.

A voice I know struggles through the underwater voices.

"Chase. You have to—" Garbling groans cut Bal off. He fades in and out. "—wake up—"

The groans morph into real voices. And the

more I listen, the more I pick up on the deep chirpings.

The Guards are here. They've come to take me away. Be it to Aben or the Hole, doesn't matter. Both equal THE END in thick, black capital letters. Maybe Aben really wants me to be his Scout— whatever that truly is. Maybe he doesn't want to extinguish me. Maybe, but if Bal is telling the truth…

"—wake up *now*, Chase!"

"Dude," I say (not even sure he can hear me). "I've never done this before. Lay off a little, jerkwad."

"Don't think," Bal shouts (ah, so he *can* hear me). "Go. Hurry!"

Is he really yelling at me right now? Seriously? He's the one who got me into this crazy mess in the first place. And if I want to get all technical about it, I wouldn't even be here if not for him. Remind him of his son or not, I'd probably be enjoying a nice, peaceful After if he—

A huge section of the wall in front of me rolls up, revealing a hole that looks to be roughly the size of a VW Beetle. A round window.

It's blurry at first, as if someone ran a bar of soap over it several times. Then the view clears and I'm staring at Bal's black, nondescript face. He glances to the right, looks at me again. His white eyes are practically bulging.

Holy crowpoop! I'm looking through the unit's

eyes.

"Now walk. I unstrapped the unit. Go through the Dock. I'm going to try to hold them off for you."

Everything is happening so fast, though one detail occurs to me.

"I need to get Sara. She——"

"No time, Chase. Get to that Dock and be quick about it."

"Listen, I can——"

"No! For the love of Death, get your smartass through and don't look back."

"What about you? What about Sara?"

But Bal slips away from my sight. A little further away I hear him say, "We need Aben. I can't get him out of the unit."

"Head Warden," chirps a Guard, "is on his way."

"Good. That's good."

"We are. Instructed. To bring. Unit. To him."

"I tried moving him, but nothing happens. I think he locked the unit down somehow. Maybe..."

Okay, enough of that. I need to get this unit's butt in gear. But... how the hell am I supposed to do that? It seems like forever ago since being in my body. And I *grew up* in that body. Knew all the ins and outs.

But this unit...

This unit is different. The more I probe around, the more I realize this. Still, I think the mechanics of walking are the same. Should be anyway.

I lift my leg a bit, step forward. Nothing. Hmm.

I think, *WALK*, in huge black letters. A forceful command.

The view through the large window shifts, steadies again. Shifts some more, steadies.

Ha. Okay. Now we're getting somewhere.

Dock 1 is only a couple feet ahead. Then the unit stops.

"What the," I manage before the unit resumes walking. Slow, steady, lame. I huff. "Jumpin' toad shit, don't *do* that to me."

Not too far away, a Guard shouts, "It's moving! Get it!"

Bal says, "Careful. Might be a trick!"

A bunch of clattering noises fills the unit's head. They're coming. Bal's attempt at holding them off fails.

Shit.

WALK FASTER.

The unit's slow sway quickens. The wavering, black rectangle goes from being feet away to merely inches. I laugh. Even if this is so weird, it's kinda cool too. There might not be the even-flow connection my real body and I shared, but there is, at least, a connection here. Don't ask me how, but there is.

Swift, heavy boots on the conveyer shake the body I'm in.

They're so close. All they have to do is reach out and...

The unit steps into Dock 1, and into the black.

A moment of extreme vertigo hits. Then… the fog.

~ 4 ~

A CAPERING MADNESS OF various shades of gray. A storm of absolute confusion.

A man's voice rises out of it all. "I'm here to make your dream come true, Andi."

An all too familiar voice.

The fog shifts, opens enough to reveal a sheet of paper with the header, Binding Contract, emblazoned in shimmery black letters. The same slender hand that once held a scalpel now holds a fountain pen. Black ink drips from the tip, splats onto the lower right corner of the paper, and slithers off onto the table. Sight flicks away from the strangeness, returning to the contract.

The familiar voice, "You will have all you ever wanted. All you've ever dreamed. Sign and live that dream, sweet girl. It's what your brother would want for you."

A girl's voice, "Chase…"

"Yesss."

The tip of the fountain pen scratches across the bottom

portion of the contract. The signature writhes, as though alive. Maybe it is. A large, manicured hand pulls the contract out of view.

"You made the right choice, Andi."

"W-who are you again?"

A slight chuckle. "Aben. And I'm here to make your dream come true. Your very own bod-mod shop, and you open tomorrow, so I suggest you get some rest."

The foggy storm blasts in, obliterating the scene. Voices become muffled grumbles. Then——

I'm awake inside a body, watching the gray fogs evaporate, and thinking, *Aben, you son of a bitch.* If that all really happened or is happening, he's messing with my baby sister. Not cool.

Waking up in a body is slow. I've forgotten how friggin' slow it is.

Oh, I'm awake, kinda, but this damn lazy-ass bag of bones is taking its own sweet time. The brain synapses barely light up. A thin veil of fog swirls through the room, or whatever you want to call it. The place inside the body now occupied by my… consciousness? Soul?

I sit up, blinking in the dimness. The only thing passing for lighting is a somber yellow, making the moving fog look creepy and sickening. Like floating puke that'll eat me alive.

I try brightening it up but… nope.

The unit is too out of it. Too sick and worn for me to get stuff going again. A machine on Stand-By mode.

So... I sit, and wait.

I don't remember it being this way in *my* body. Then again, we were one. Happens when you're born into your destined body. Your home of all homes until it dies.

Possession is lame in comparison and I wonder why anyone (or thing) would even consider it. Trained or not. To freak the living out, maybe? But what's the purpose of the units being built in the Factory? Surely, it's more than just scaring people.

My only guess is: to infiltrate and eventually destroy humanity.

Are the Wardens creating an army? Yeah, looks that way.

My thoughts turn from the Factory to Sara. Is she okay? Has Aben already extinguished her? God, I hope not. I hope she's all right. I need to go back and get her. How selfish am I to just leave her there? Should've made Bal let me bring her to the Docks. No time to do that? Bullshit. There's always time.

I already miss her. And when I figure out how to go back...

I'm pacing the small, foggy space when the lights first strobe, then brighten. Full white. Every shadow vanishes. The fog sinks into the floor. Gone.

Well, happy day. The body is waking up. The brain sparks and crackles around me. Not on all cylinders yet, but getting there.

The huge window flutters open, clears, and I

gape at the night sky. The deepest black sprinkled with winking stars. This is the sky I remember from what feels like forever ago. Nights camping at Guile Lake in northern Iowa. Nights simply sitting outside and talking with friends. Nights alone, lying in dew-damp grass just zoning out. It's amazing, the night sky. Funny how we forget the simplest things.

A few seconds pass, then something else finds me like dozens of snakes coiling up my legs. Chilly air rises, eventually buffeting me from all directions, until the room is like a damn refrigerator.

Ah, yes. This I also forgot.

Senses.

It's cold outside, and the unit feels it. If we wait too long, it'll slip into hypothermia. Need to get our asses in gear.

Okay. Let's do this then.

I say, "Stand."

Nothing. The sky remains still.

The body begins to shiver. The lights dim, brighten, dim.

Oh, for the love of—

STAND.

The view tilts drastically. The body sits, then stands. Now I see an old woodshed, barely visible in the dark, in front of me. A gray ruin surrounded by dead weeds.

Not much, but it'll have to do. Shelter is shelter. The weeds are wet with dew and practically freezing. Which makes everything so much more miserable.

WALK.

The unit moves forward a couple steps. The view sways drastically back and forth. A clicking noise sounds and I concentrate on *BALANCE*.

Nothing happens. We're going to fall.

BALANCE, you meat puppet.

The view straightens and stills. At least we didn't go down right away. Gives me time to correct things. Thank cheese pizza for small favors.

We're still aimed for the shed. Which is also a plus.

WALK. I add, *SLOW*, for good measure.

And... off we go.

The vision sways steadily. So much so, it's barely noticeable.

Good deal.

The woodshed's door is shut. If it's locked, we're screwed. This body will either die overnight or get severely ill from so much exposure.

It's not, like, really cold out. Probably the lower forties by the feel. But still, the unit is naked and as sensitive as a newborn baby. Doesn't take much to hurt them when they come directly off the line.

Or so I've overheard a few times.

I focus on the door latch. No knob. Just an eight inch, black strip of steel and a heavy-duty clip for it to latch into. Lift up, and the door is open. Push down, it latches. Easy peasie.

And—well shit—will you look at this. No

padlock on the latch.

I send the words: *GRAB LATCH*, to the unit's brain.

Somewhere deeper in, a brief whooshing sound rises and falls. Motor skills? Probably.

Finally, a hand reaches into view, grasps the steel latch, retracts. The fingers splay wide in surprise.

The steel is cold, but not *that* cold. Jeez.

GRAB LATCH, I repeat and add, *HOLD*.

Once more, the hand grips the latch. I wait for the unit's senses to retract again, but this time the hand stays put. Every nerve thrums, telling the body: No! Let go! That's *cold*! Good thing my will goes beyond the senses.

Heavy shivers wrack the unit. The heart speeds up a few notches.

Okie-dokie, time to get moving.

LIFT LATCH.

The hand lifts the latch, lowers it.

Face-palm.

Jesus hopping on a lily-pad, *really*?

I must've possessed a defective unit because this is getting ridonkulous. There's a damn brain, why is it so… well, stupid? I mean, I get the body is fresh off the line. Doesn't know any more than what the Programmers installed. But still…

"All right, dimwit," I say. "Pay attention this time."

LIFT LATCH. HOLD. OPEN DOOR.

Thankfully, the unit does as it's told. Though the

entire arm is a trembling mess with all the shivers passing through.

The door to the woodshed squeals open. Nothing but pitch blackness inside. This alone pauses me for a moment.

When you live in some otherworldly place called the Factory filled with all sorts of terrifying monsters, you always stop and think before entering the dark. Never know what's lurking inside. Waiting. Face split in a huge, hungry grin. Ready to dig its hot claws in and eat, eat, eat.

But this isn't the Factory, nor the world that horrible place runs in.

This is Earth. My world. The only monsters here are the human ones.

This too stops me from entering the shed. Might be some psycho in there. I woke him up and now he's got his knife out and—

"Jesus," I growl. "You're freaking yourself out. Knock it off, pull up your diaper and get inside."

And now... I'm talking to myself.

I send, *WALK INSIDE.*

The unit hesitates. A tiny whine sounds from somewhere in the brain. A fear sensor, maybe? Hell, probably. Guess I don't blame it for being tripped.

I repeat: *WALK INSIDE.*

We step into the darkness. The body turns to the open doorway without command. A reflex. No doubt wanting to bolt out of here. But we have to take a chance. If there is anything in the shed waiting to eat us, then that's that. Game over. Nothing I can do about it.

SHUT DOOR.

The unit takes hold of the inside latch, pulls door shut. A low, stuttering squeal fills the small space. The latch falls in place with a metallic, *click*.

Full darkness.

I turn the unit around and we move a few cautious steps further into the shed. Careful not to trip over anything hiding in all this black. Feeling sensors on the feet pick up grittiness, and splintery floorboards. The floor itself is chilly, but not wet and cold like the weeds and grass outside. So this is a plus. It's dry.

The unit's right big toe thumps against something hard. Pain zings up the leg to the brain and back down again.

Damn, that hurt. Everything the unit feels, I feel. We're fully connected now, it seems. Not sure if this is a good or bad thing. Not melded, yet, but if that happens we're stuck together.

We stop. Hot tears fill the unit's eyes and the darkness in front of me gets all swimmy. I have to remind myself that this body isn't yet hardened to pain. It's extremely sensitive. So, cursing at it for being a wimp is kinda mean. I do so anyway. Not trying to be mean, just angry. Pissed off about all of this. Yeah, I'm out of the Factory. I'm back on Earth. But so what? This body is all weird. Maybe *too* sensitive. Something about it screams *different* to me. Not sure what that means, but the feeling is constant.

And so far, no monsters—human or otherwise—attack us. The shed is empty. Of course it is. There aren't monsters *everywhere*. Sometimes we just freak ourselves out for no reason at all. Like the five-year-old that knows without knowing there's something in his closet. Sometimes it's nothing at all. Sometimes…

The pain eases, but never really goes away. Stubbed that toe pretty damn good.

I make the unit back up a little and then bend and feel around. We need a blanket or tarp, or anything that will cover us from the chill. Shelter is good, but this body needs to warm up a little. Eventually our hand sweeps across something stiff, though undoubtedly cloth. Not sure how far into the shed when we find this. Maybe near the back.

PICK UP.

The unit does and, by the feel sensors, I discover it's not what I'd hoped for—a blanket. Too short. Too thin. I think it's a towel.

It'll have to do.

I find us a spot with less splinters and command the body to lie down. It follows orders and soon we're flat on our back, stiff towel covering our torso from neck to groin. Not much, but it is warming the body up by a couple degrees, so this works for me. The arms and legs are still cold, but that's all right. The main thing is to keep the core warm.

Drowsiness thickens the air in this tiny room I live in. The fog returns, rising from the floor like magic.

Uh-oh.

Sleep isn't good right now. Need to let the body warm up a bit. If sleep comes now, a coma might work its way in. And that'd suck stinky feet.

My efforts to keep the unit awake fail. It drifts away, pulling me along into oblivion.

A dark river to nowhere.

And I'm stuck in it.

Oddly enough, I'm not asleep or at rest. I'm fully awake and thinking about the weird visions/dreams that have been popping up lately. They're of Andi. I know that much. And Aben had her sign a contract. But what was all that about dreams coming true and owning her own bod-mod shop? I didn't know she liked that stuff. Unless her tastes changed from classical art to modern art involving skin and body parts and such. Which is cool, but… damn, how long have I been gone?

The unit needs to wake up. It's naked, for the love of chunky peanut butter. And if day has come, maybe I'll be able to find something—a gunny sack probs—to cover up with until I can steal some real clothes.

My agenda is simple.

Find clothes. Eat. Drink. Fuel up the body. Find

Mom and Andi. Then... disappear.

I've decided the Obsidious isn't my problem. I'm no hero.

Screw trying to save humanity. It's doomed anyway. With all the nit-picky wars and hair triggers, all the politically correct bullshit, all the selfish, self-centered a-holes populating this world...

They'll kill themselves off eventually. Sooner rather than later if they don't get their shit together. Which, I fear, they never will. They've fallen from grace in so many ways, and now tumble in an ever-turning downward spiral.

So why should I care about them?

I shouldn't. Yet, there's this faint sting in my center. A painful urge to at least *try* to help.

I dunno. Maybe it's the human residue still flowing through me. Or maybe it's Andi. Yeah, more likely her. Maybe get her and Mom to hole up with me until the Obsidious does its damage and things clear off. We might be the only human beings left, but oh well. Can't be helped.

The large window of the unit's vision opens. I gape at a ceiling dotted with tiny pin-pricks of light. Thin strings of sun shoot down like mini sabers. Holes in the roof, which looks like tin, maybe.

The cold is mostly gone, thank the gods of purple elephants. There's that at least.

The unit's eyes shift back and forth, but all I see are old, gray rafters and the pin-pricks of sunlight.

SIT UP.

The unit does.

Okie dokie. Let's see what we can see.

Looking around in the dull light, dust floats and twirls in thin rays of sun. There's a mixture of smells coming in now. Above all, the sour stench of damp wood. Add in dashes of oil, gasoline, dirt, and you get this not so unpleasant aroma. Reminds me a bit of my grandpa's old dirt floor garage. A nostalgic smell.

A stack of split wood rests at the back of the shed, gray and neglected. Above this is a warped shelf. I spy an elderly can of WD-40. What might be a box of matches. And—well, shit—a friggin' chainsaw. Very old one, judging by the rust that cakes the chain and teeth. The faded and chipped away orange paint on the body reveals heavy use from its past. Now it's nothing but a relic in this small, dim shed. Rotting away like everything else trapped in here.

Nothing I can use. And I doubt the matches even light anymore.

Along the right wall on rusty nails hang a scoop shovel, a spade shovel, and one of those long-bladed things that the all-too-real Grim Reaper is said to appear with.

What the hell are those called?

Scythe?

I think that's right.

On the floor, another neat stack of ancient wood. Two large, wooden crates lay in front of the stack. Tops open.

Maybe there's something useful in these. Maybe. Damn, I hope so.

The left wall of the shed is bare. The floor, on the other hand, is littered with four smaller wooden crates—one of these we no doubt stubbed our toe on last night—, a gas can with peeling red paint, a plastic jug of some strange black liquid, and a pair of tired-looking, brown leather work boots.

The owner must've switched from shoes to boots when he came to the shed, or whatever.

I mean, what exactly is this place? For a woodshed, there's barely any wood. Just a couple of small stacks.

Still, the boots might be of some use.

All right, enough gawking.

STAND.

It takes a bit of effort, but the unit gains its feet. We shuffle to one of the smaller crates and peer inside.

Tools. Old, rusty, friggin' *tools.*

Next crate.

Beady black eyes stare up at me. I retreat a little. I mean, what the *hell?* Jeez. Then I take another gander inside.

The owner of the beady black eyes is a damn Teddy Bear. Its fake, tan fur is matted with filth and worn by time. It's missing the right arm. Stuffing— turned gray over an unknown amount of years— pokes out like a tiny storm cloud. Mouse droppings sprinkle the top of Mr. Bear and the gritty, dust laden bottom of the crate surrounding it. And between the stubby, matted legs, I find the culprit. Well… what's left of it anyway.

The mouse is mostly just fur and bones. The eye sockets where tiny oil-drop eyes used to be are now empty black holes that lead directly to Death himself.

The unit shivers massively.

I follow suit.

Something creepy as hell about this. Creepy, and sad. Indeed, the sorrow laps at me in lazy waves. A constant sadness. Not for the mouse, really, but for Mr. Bear. So out of place in this old shed, with its rusty tools and gray cords of elderly wood.

Then again, maybe the owner of the shed brought his kid here and said kid forgot his or her Teddy Bear. Maybe the owner tossed it the crate, thinking he'll take it back home with him after work is finished. Maybe…

We move to the final small crate.

Ah, here we go.

I make the unit reach in and pull out a faded, green raincoat. It's silly as hell, but so far it's my only option. Unless…

I send us to the larger crates on the right side of the shed, and—holy shit—the first one, it's packed with neatly folded *clothes*. Real, honest to goodness cl

—

The unit's eyes focus. All I can do is stand here

and gape at we're seeing.

Neatly folded, yes, but—what is *this*?

On top is a blue t-shirt. Well, *mostly* blue. Black mold creeps around the viewable sleeve. But that's not what catches my attention and holds it. There are several large brownish blotches near the collar area. That's *not* mold.

My first thought is: *Why is there poop all the way up there?*

Then I think: *That's not poop…*

Reach down and pick up the shirt. It unfolds. A small cloud of dust plumes. This triggers the unit to sneeze a couple times. When I lift the shirt into full view, even the unit gasps.

The entire front of the small blue shirt is bibbed with the brown stuff. Brown, because the shirt is blue. Because the liquid that created the stains has long since dried. But the liquid isn't originally brown. It's red. And this is what my mind sees now, the brown becoming red. So blinding in its bluntness. Red. So much of it spells DEATH in gaudy neon letters.

It's clear. The kid who wore this shirt—a boy—is now dead. And the result wasn't natural. A monster ushered this death. Possibly the worst kind of monster ever.

Drop the shirt. It plops onto the neatly folded pile. More dust plumes. The unit sneezes. Pick up another piece of clothing. This time it's a small, yellow summer dress. The blotches here are dark crimson. Red…

"*Shit*," I manage.

Drop the dress and back away. We shoot glances around the shed. A slick lump forms in our throat. I make the unit swallow it down before it catches the gag reflex's attention. The last thing I want right now is to be dry heaving. The unit is running on empty. No food or water in our stomach.

Valuable saliva fills our mouth and this too I force us to swallow.

The units are always pumped full of a solution to keep them hydrated for twenty-four hours. I dunno if this one received the solution. If so, it doesn't have much longer.

After a moment, the urge to puke passes, thank gods of antipukedom.

I begin to see what the real purpose of this old shed is. This dark spot in the world. Our vision picks up details we missed before.

Beside the woodpile in the back is a dirty tarp. Something brownish is caked on it. Something that was red before it was brown. Blood. Dark stains sweep the warped boards of the floor here and there. And when I cast the unit's eyes back to the smaller crate with all those tools…

That's not just rust covering them.

The place is a shed of horrors. Some sick bastard brought kids here. Kids that'll never grow up. Never know what it's like to kiss a girl or boy. Never know what paths lie in wait for them to follow in life. The choices, good and bad, they must make as the years fly by, closer and closer to Death's open, bony arms.

An icy chill slithers through the unit, finds its way to me. I shiver in unison.

I don't really want to, but it needs to be done. There has to be something more than an old raincoat and dead kid's clothes. We peer into the second large box. I immediately wish we hadn't. Because what's in box number two is something that'll probably haunt my dreams forever.

More than a dozen small skulls stare up at me with dark, empty eye sockets. Each one with its own thin layer of dust.

"Jesus," I gasp and we back away.

A sorrow so deep it penetrates to the inner core of the unit. The walls, they turn a somber blue. A cold breeze lifts and falls. The air gets heavy. Yeah. It has this weird weight to it I can't fully understand. All I know is it's here and I hate it. Want it to go away. This isn't only the unit's sadness, but the sadness of many children still stuck in this old, rotting tomb. Not ghosts, really, but their final hurts and sorrows before Death arrived. Their lingering emotions.

I do the only thing I can think of.

Grab the raincoat and boots, and get the hell out of the shed as the sun dips below the horizon.

FINDING ANDI

~ 1 ~

Okay, so maybe the raincoat was a bad idea.

The body's core temperature crawls higher and higher as we navigate through trash congested alleyways. Sweat creates irritating squeaks at the crooks of our elbows. The view through the unit's eyes gets all wavy from time to time. If it isn't one thing it's another with this friggin' body.

And as night melds to another day, there's the stink. Probably the worst body odor I've ever encountered.

We need some damn antiperspirant. *Phew.*

Well, I'll be damned if I wear some dead kid's clothes. That's just beyond horrible.

Then again, is wearing the garment of a monster any better?

Either way, it's craziness to the tenth power.

Gotta find some real clothes before someone notices us and starts asking questions. Before shit hits the fan, in other words.

A few syringes crunch under the heels of the monster's boots. Probably heroin junkies leaving their crap behind. Then again, for all I know there's someone with a serious case of diabetes living around here.

Vehicles blat their horns. People jabber into their phones—though most are texting. Heads down, staring at the small screens, they somehow manage to avoid bumping into anyone or any thing... or step into traffic and get splattered.

Zombie-like they might be, but they are also oblivious of the stranger in the raincoat as we move out of yet another alley.

Maybe they're desensitized enough that seeing someone in an old raincoat and decaying work boots slinking out of an alley isn't very out of place. I knew society was getting bad, but this is totally wonkynuts.

They see us, but don't at the same time. Like we're a scurrying sewer rat in the gutter. They know it's there. They see it, but ignore it anyway. Pretend it doesn't really exist and maybe it'll go away.

Oh well, doesn't hurt my feelings any. Getting noticed is the last thing I want.

I work us out of downtown and into one of the surrounding residential communities. A suburb, kinda. Hawthorn isn't a huge enough city for real suburbs. Nothing like Chicago or New York. Think more like Des Moines, or Minneapolis. Not giant, but close enough.

I should know; I lived in this falling apart town before Dad decided to punch me just a little too hard in the wrong spot of my head. Not sure where, but I assume in the temple. All I know is it was *bam*, lights out. Then I'm on the Path to my destined After.

There's a reason why I'm sneaking through this small residential area. Houses are easier to steal from than retail stores. Plain and simple. Stores, they're choked with people and cameras, and alarms. Granted, some houses have security systems, but at least my chances are greater coming away with something and not getting my ass hauled to juvi.

All I have to do is find an older house.

It's sometime in the early afternoon. The sun blasts its glare on this tiny section of the world. Judging by the cold last night, I'm guessing it's spring. Like its brother, fall, its temperatures are bi-polar. Probably the middle of May, but who the hell knows. All I know is the unit is overheating in this friggin' raincoat. The sweatier we get, the noisier the squeaks. We're dehydrating fast.

Residential areas might be easier to steal from, but the people here are more aware of people and things that don't belong. All it takes is one person and things'll get sour in a hurry.

So I keep to the thick bushes, wriggle through filthy crawlspaces with houses that have them, and hide in trees from the occasional kid or passer-by.

All this wears the unit out more quickly. We need food and water. Fuel. Energy.

Food and water first. Clothes second.

Just have to find a...

I peek through a side window into a small ranch style home. I wait. Wait some more. No sign of life inside other than a super fat cat with a barely visible pink collar winking through black fur. No dog as far as I can tell. Man, I hope there's no dog. Dogs are too vocal. Run across the wrong one, too, and it'll rip you to shreds.

We slink to the back door of the house, glance around.

Coming together quite quickly, this unit and I. Not sure if that's a good or bad thing.

The neighborhood echoes with the sounds of kids playing. School must be out already. A couple dogs bark a few times. Birds sing their songs. Just your typical suburbia sounds. Kinda comforting, actually. Most important, though, there aren't any gawkers. I'm alone for the time being.

The door opens without trouble. Another plus; some people either forget or don't lock their doors.

We hurry inside and close the door.

Just beyond the door is a mud room. Here I stop and listen for any signs that I'm not alone in the house. Peeking in a window is just that. You only get a view of a room, maybe two, and can't hear much.

The only sound is a lazy, yet consistent, *tick-tick-*

tick. No TV. No radio.

Together, we let go a long breath.

Either the owner of this silent house is taking a nap, or they're gone for now. I hope it's the latter.

Need to get moving.

We pass through a small, but tidy kitchen. Judging by the modern appliances and iPhone chargers plugged into the wall near a stainless steel toaster, this might be the home of a younger couple. Maybe. These days, it seems, even the elderly have friggin' iPhones.

Next room is a quaint dining room, or whatever it is. There's no table. No China hutch. But there's an old looking grandfather clock. Its golden pendulum sways back and forth, back and forth, *tick-tick-tick*.

In one corner is a pink pet bed. Not quite large enough for a dog.

For Sir Kitty, most likely.

Atop an end-table are two photos. One is a weeding picture. A man and woman, possibly in their middle twenties, smile the biggest smiles I think I've ever seen. A happy moment captured forever. Well, until the photo fades over time. Although, that might be pretty much forever anyway.

The other photo is of the same smiling couple standing in front of a ranch style house. *This* house, in fact.

Well, all right. Solves the question of whose

house it is. Thank god. Would've sucked fuzzy donkey balls to wear some old dude's clothes.

The guy in the photo doesn't appear too tall. He's slender, but not gangly. About the same as the unit I saw on the Dock. Good. Finally, things are beginning to get a little easier.

Moments later, I hesitate before entering the couple's bedroom. Struck by a sudden shock of worry, I stand in the doorway. It's almost like I'm sneaking into my parents' room to check out Dad's extensive collection of Playboy. I'm going into a private place reserved for the owners of the house. I'm going to steal some of the dude's clothes. And I shouldn't be here. It's wrong. Not me. But here's the thing, I have to do this. Might be my only chance. I have to, for Andi and Mom.

Plus, the unit simply can't continue in this raincoat for much longer. Heatstroke will end it and I'll be stuck inside until the body dies. and when it does… then what? Will I be flung back onto my Path? Or—

Enough. I'm not sure when Mr. and Mrs. Big Smiles will be back. Gotta get this done.

I find a nice pair of jeans in the third large drawer of the dresser. Size 31. Should be perfect. If not, there has to be a belt around here somewhere. On the opposite side of the drawer are a bunch of folded t-shirts. It's like striking gold when I find a black band shirt. My favorite band, actually.

Slipknot. Them badasses from Iowa. My home

state.

Toss the shirt on the bed with the jeans.

Probably better check out the underwear situation.

Top drawer of the dresser is split in half. On the right, her stuff. On the left is his. All boxer-briefs. No tightie-whities, thank all the gods and maple syrup. There are also socks in this drawer. Two for one. Hells yeah.

The unit's stomach grumbles. A low bubbling. Slight discomfort. We're starving. The body needs nourishment. But what if Mr. and Mrs. Big Smiles come back while we're pigging out in their kitchen? What do I say? "Oh, hey you guys. Sorry I broke into your home and stole your clothes and ate all the leftovers, but I'm from a parallel world and I've come to save my sister and mom from this thing called the Obsidious, and well… you see this body isn't really mine but it needs—"

Yeah. No. That'd be bad. Really bad.

An errant thought passes through my mind, but only briefly. I *could* go home and wear my own clothes, but what if Mom tossed them out or gave them to some consignment shop, or something? Also, I'm in this different body. It'll take a lot of convincing for her to believe it's really me, anyway. *A lot*.

Even then, she might not believe. No matter how many facts I throw at her, she'll be dubious. Andi might get it, but Mom? Shit, I dunno.

We grab the clothes and hurry to a conjoining bathroom. There's a faint whiff of some kind of fruity shampoo or soap. I note the shower and dismiss it. I can wash the body later, maybe. Hopefully.

Taking the raincoat off is like peeling away another layer of skin. Not easy, kinda hurts, and the stink of the unit's body odor gags even me. Definitely need a shower soon. Until then I'll just have to use the man's deodorant and cologne. In any case, I'm glad as hell to be rid of that damned raincoat. The garment of a child killer.

Drop the raincoat, kick off the boots and bend to put on the underwear when something odd slips across our peripheral vision. Something in the mirror above the sink. Our reflection, I'm sure, but...

Sometimes mirrors are rifts to other worlds, or pockets in time. Sometimes creatures from these other worlds find themselves at the rift. On their side it might be a pond, or a shiny piece of metal, or whatever. And sometimes these slobbering horrors slip into this world.

Learned this while at the Factory, and it scared me knowing how truly thin the membranes between worlds are.

I straighten the body and gaze at the large mirror.

Blink.

"Um..." is all I can manage.

What. The. Shit? This can't be right.

I command the unit to lift our arms. In the mirror we do. Lower the arms and stare.

Indeed, there's a creature staring back at us, but it's far from a slobbering horror. Made in a different world, sure, but nothing as scary.

Now it all makes sense. No wonder the unit feels so weird, so different. No wonder Bal freaked out when I possessed the unit. He realized I jumped into the wrong one.

Instead of a monster or a dude, a human girl gapes at me. A teenage girl. Her face is an extraordinary work of art. Almost completely altered by a black and white tattoo that covers the entire face like a mask.

Whoever drew this has to be one of the greatest artists around. All the white obviously represents dead skin. Black stitches run from the top of the forehead to the very nub of the chin, and horizontally across, just above the brow; creating an obscure cross. The closer I look, the more I pick out green and gray hues for shadows where the "skin" stretches with the pull of the fake stitches. So the effect is pretty close to real.

Her hair is black, long and beyond messy. It's like a squirrel has been up there rooting around. Her earlobes are gauged, but nothing extreme. Maybe a couple millimeters, give or take. The arms though… they twist with horrible burn marks. Yet, as I inspect these closer I notice they're not just burn marks, but designs etched into the skin. What do they call this? Branding?

Hell, I dunno. The designs are interesting. Like abstract paintings, they give off more emotion than anything clear cut. To most they don't make sense because they are unidentifiable. These are the folks who see the trees before the forest. The unimaginative.

Our sight lowers and—

"Holy shit," I say. "I have boobs!"

And do I! Wow. I lift the unit's hands towards them. Not sure why. To feel them, I guess. Yet, in this moment something changes in the unit. An electrical charge slaps me across the face.

"Ow," I cry. "Hey, what the—"

We aren't looking at our boobs anymore. In the mirror, our stitched face furrows into the deepest frown I've ever seen. There's a really good word for this sort of frown, but... what?

Glower. Yes, that's it! She's glowering.

Yeah, okay, fine, but it's not me doing this. The unit... she's glowering on her own. Using the mirror to get the point across. As if to say: Yes, you, asshole. Those are *my* boobs.

"Whoa," I say. "Chill. Not like I chose you on purpose."

Another electrical slap rocks me on my heels.

"Jesus jellybeans, *really*? What the hell was *that* for?"

She doesn't respond, of course. Nor does her

tatted face change. The same disdainful glower remains.

She's waking up. Her conscience anyway. I guess the phenomenon is rare, and the units that show signs of it are usually disposed of in the Factory. Too much for the possessor to deal with. This is if it's caught before deployment, though. Not sure how they deal with such an issue in the field.

Anyway, the fact remains, she didn't like me trying to cop a feel.

Guess that's understandable and all, but what now? Is there going to be some kind of power struggle to see who controls us? And if she wins…?

Gradually her face slackens. The electrical buzzing stops. She's falling back to sleep, I think. I hope so. That was some weird shit. After a while there's no sense of her. Coast is clear. Phew.

I dress us in the guy's clothes. If she doesn't like it, oh friggin' well.

Pad back into the bedroom. Shoes. I need sneakers. Running shoes. Anything besides those giant, ugly boots. But all I find are a pair of really shiny black dress shoes and black stilettos.

Eh… nope.

Grab the raincoat and boots and go downstairs.

The clock on the microwave reads: 4:03 pm.

Assuming Mr. and Mrs. Big Smiles work regular day shift hours (9am to 5pm), I have time to eat. Barely.

There's a pair of women's running shoes beside

the front door, and a pair of the dude's Doc Marten's. I try the Docs on first, and my center sinks. Of course they're too big. I'm a damn teenage girl with stupid tiny feet. Sigh.

The running shoes fit almost perfectly. Pink and black. Oh, joy. Ugh.

I return to the kitchen and open the refrigerator. And, bingo.

A red and white pizza box rests on the center shelf. Pull the box out, place it on the counter. I just hope to Christ it doesn't have mushrooms. I hate—

It's a half pie of pepperoni!

Not my favorite but—Woo-Hoo!

I dig in.

I'm so into eating the cold pizza I barely hear the footsteps sneaking up behind me.

Too late to move.

Giant claws spin us around with so much force the unit's spine crackles and pops. We're thrown off balance. Might have cracked our head a good one on the floor if one of the huge claws didn't latch onto our throat and lift us into the air.

A rumbling growl fills the unit's head.

And when the vision clears from disorientation, I stare directly into the elongated, pale face of Aben's Ik.

How…?

My light blasts strobes throughout my tiny inner room as terror rips through us. The Ik opens its maw, revealing lots of jagged teeth and a hideously long, gray tongue that flaps and lashes at me. A deep hiss sounds. Reminds me of what an alligator or crocodile sounds like on one of those nature shows.

Then the maw snaps shut. The claw choking us releases and we drop to the floor hard enough to make our teeth click together. Pain shrieks through the unit before finally falling to a dull murmur.

It looms over us, the Ik. Its narrow chest expands, deflates, expands, deflates. A runner of yellowish drool oozes down its grotesque chin. But it doesn't attack. Doesn't move. Weird. I think if it wanted to kill me it would've done so already. Maybe—

The Ik's maw opens again, only this time instead of a hiss or growl, a very familiar voice says, "This is *not* what I'd call disappearing, Chase."

Within my tiny room, I blink. The unit does the same.

"Bal?"

The Ik's narrow black eyes roll. "Yes. Of course it's me. Who else would it be?"

We sit up, the unit and I, and rub our lower back. "Sure coulda fooled me, man. Thought you were one of Aben's minions."

A grunt escapes the gaping maw, then—

"He sent this creature after me once he found out I betrayed him."

"So... you possessed it?"

"I cannot fight an Ik, Chase. They're too strong.

My only defense was to possess it and get out of the Factory."

I imagine the girl unit frowning as I do. "How'd you find me?"

"We're linked. It happens when a Counselor picks a soul off their Path. Anywhere you go, I'll know. But if I can find you so easily, so can Aben. He has the power to tap into such things."

I get the unit back on her feet. The throbbing pain in our lower back worsens a bit before fading. I try to ignore Bal's swampy odor. This is a task all its own, but I manage all right.

"Well, I needed food and clothes, man," I say. "What I found in that shed was… bad."

"Shed?" Bal says. "Oh yes. That. The working place of Fred Kinnick. Child murderer. He was never caught, you know."

"That's messed up," I say. "Why the hell would you send me there, of all places?"

The Ik shrugs. "Every Dock leads to some dark spot in the world. More energy in such places. You possessed the wrong unit and went through the wrong Dock anyway."

"Well which friggin' one was I supposed to go through? You never told me which—"

"Never mind. It's done. But now you'll need to be more careful." Bal is quiet for a bit, then adds. "I know you want your mother and sister to go with you, but I assure you that's a mistake. Here is my advice, and I'm telling you it's the only way. Flee north. As far as you can go. The Obsidious spores don't survive well in extreme cold. Aben's reach doesn't fare well in the cold either. Go as far as you can and wait until I find you. If you stay here, Aben will locate you and destroy you."

Yeah, so I'm pretty speechless. How the hell is someone supposed to respond to all that? Damn. It takes me a little while, but finally my mind grasps on something.

"Dude, if we go too far north we'll freeze to death." Petty, but it's all I've got.

"There's a backpack in an abandoned house on the east side of town. It's full of money. A thief hid it not long before he was caught and imprisoned."

Blink. "Really?"

The Ik nods.

"Would've been nice to know *before* I left the Factory, jerkface."

Bal says again, "You took the wrong Dock. Anyway, go there now and use the money for clothes and weather gear and transportation. I have to go back for now, but I'll find you."

Before I have time to rebut, the Ik turns and flickers out of existence. Well, hell, it'd be nice to be able to do *that*.

I finish up the rest of the cold pizza, drink two Cokes back to back, and a glass of water. Grab two bottles of water. Then I leave the house of Mr. and Mrs. Big Smiles.

Despite what Bal says, I gotta find my family.

~ 2 ~

BAL CAN STICK HIS advice right up his narrow nonexistent ass. Disappear? Go north? Sure, but not without Mom and Andi. He's got to realize that. Maybe he does. I dunno.

If Aben really is coming for me we need to get this over with.

About a half hour is all it takes. The sky is pretty much getting over the whole twilight thing. Night is like right here. Almost.

It's different, my house. Not like drastically, but those shrubs in front flanking the porch weren't there when my body died. The siding is different too. Instead of white, it's baby powder blue now.

So, Mom fixed the place up a little. So what? I'm just happy I'm here and Dad is most likely in prison.

Okay. Here goes. Gotta prepare myself for instant rejection. Prepare to throw out stuff only I'd know before the door slams in our face. That's if

Mom even answers the door. Might take one look out the window and shake her head.

We mount the porch and stop in front of the door. Draw in a breath, blow it out. Knock. I wait. Nothing. Knock again.

I'm about to go to the back door when I hear someone from inside the house shout, "Be right there."

Is it Mom? Kinda sounds like her. But I dunno how long I've been gone so maybe it's Andi. She was fourteen when Dad killed my body. Out of the two, though, I hope it's her.

The door opens, and the smile I put on the unit's tatted face melts.

The woman in the doorway is neither Mom nor Andi. What the…

The woman is short, in her late thirties, maybe, with dark hair tied back in a messy bun. There's a curious frown forming on her cute face.

"Can I help you?" Her brown eyes flit over the unit's tattoos with what might be interest or disgust, or both.

"Um," I manage. Gaining control of my confusion I add, "I'm sorry I must have the wrong house. I'm looking for the Dunnings?"

She lifts a dark eyebrow. For a moment, she seems even more confused. Then, her face clears a little. The eyebrow lowers. A smile touches her lips.

"Yes," she says. "You have the right house, but the Dunnings no longer live here. I've lived here for two years now."

Two years? Holy crap, have I really been gone so long?

"Oh," I say as the shock wears off. "So, um, do you know where they might have moved to?"

The woman's eyes soften some as she speaks. "Well, after the son died, the father went to prison. A couple years after that, the daughter ran away and Mrs. Dunning, or so people say, went crazy. She's in Kind Hill Asylum now as far as I know."

"*What*?" It just spills out of my mouth. "Ran away—*Kind Hill*? How…"

Her features harden. "May I ask who you are? Your name? How do you know the Dunnings?"

I spin my new body around without another word. This is insane. How… why…

"Excuse me," the woman calls. "I need your name."

Yeah, right, lady.

Over the unit's shoulder I say, "Thanks for your help."

"*Wait*," she cries. "I can call someone for you. We might be able to…"

Ignoring her, we cross the street and hurry away. Not the kind of attention I need.

Bal might've been right; trying for my Mom and sister was a mistake.

Shit, I can imagine how it must've been for Mom. First her husband kills her son, then her daughter runs away. Everyone she loves just… gone.

I'd go nutty too. That's too much to deal with and I wonder how she's doing up there in Kind Hill? Are they taking care of her, or are they letting her rot (as has been rumored since the place opened somewhere in the 1920s) as the ghosts pick, pick, pick away at her?

The unit's stomach lurches. Hot saliva squirts into our mouth. Our throat swells.

And for the first time in a long time, I feel the forceful expel of vomit. The emptiness it leaves in its wake. The ache it causes in the stomach and throat. The stingy-sour stench in our nostrils.

We're on our knees at the foot of an old oak tree near the sidewalk. Half-digested pizza splatters the manicured grass. Tears fill our eyes and when we blink they cascade down our tatted face.

"Shit," I growl, wiping our chin free of a dangling mixture of spit and puke.

"Oh wow," a girl says close by. "Are you all right?"

Without looking, head still down, I say, "Go away."

Of course she doesn't.

"I can call someone if you want? Sorry, it's not every day I see someone just drop to their knees like that and puke everywhere. Kinda left field, you know?"

Shake our head. "I said get lost."

She doesn't. In fact, I can feel her pitiful gaze drilling into my back. Dammit. Leave it to me to attract the good Samaritan. Sure, she means well. She's trying to help. But, really, I don't need this sort of attention right now. What I need is to get my ass to the east side of town, find the backpack of money, find Andi, and get gone.

Closer, the girl says, "What's your name? Mine's Harper."

Wait... *Harper*? As in the girl Andi was talking to in my dream that was really not a dream and really Not Harper, but... something else? The voice is different, with a slight accent in it, but all the undertones are still there.

"Um, Jezzie," I say, and the unit's mouth snaps shut.

"Jezzie," Harper muses. Huh. Maybe she thinks it's unique? "Nice name. Are you from Hawthorn?"

If I'm right and this pretend Harper is really who I think it is, I better play it close to the chest.

"Yes," I reply, and stand. We sway as vertigo washes over us. When it passes, the sick feeling in our stomach begins fading, I keep us facing away from Harper who isn't really Harper.

I feel her curiosity seep through the unit's skin. Then the unit (by her friggin' self!) turns and here is this Not Harper. Directly in front of us. All five foot nothing of her. Cute, with short auburn hair and bronze skin. And look at all those silver studs in her ears! While other people might fall short, she totally rocks it. Her mouth lifts at the corners in an easy smile. It's the perfect suit for a monster to wear.

A monster named Ti.

Aben's right hand Warden. The deadly Queen of the Factory. Right effin' here in front of me.

But if she knows who I am she shows no sign.

I think of Sara. I'm such a selfish asshole. Should've found a way to bring her with. Maybe I can go back and get her. Somehow. I just hope Aben hasn't gotten to her yet. And about that. If Ti is here then where is Aben?

"*Love* the tatts," Not Harper says. "How old are you?"

More questions I can't answer. So I make the unit shrug. Put on a slight smirk. I gotta get out of here before she realizes I'm not just your typical girl —I mean boy.

Ti laughs in this deceptively light way and says, "Well, I love how it looks so real. Those *stitches*! All 3D. The artist must be amazing."

"Guess so," I say.

We're silent for a moment, her and I. Both gazing at each other. Her on the unit's tattoos and burn art. Me on her eyes. If they begin to darken, I have to run. There's no other choice. Yet, if she doesn't know who I am, maybe I can get close enough to kill her. If that's even possible. I dunno what Aben and Ti really are so… yeah, I just dunno. In the very least, she might take me to this Obsidious thing. Maybe if I just play along I'll get some answers without even asking.

"So," Ti says. "Where are you from? I know it's

not *this* neighborhood. But I think I remember seeing you once in school."

"Across town." A lie for a lie.

But, *face-palm.*

From here, across town means the east side. Which means, not possible. All of the places on that side are abandoned. Well, last time I knew they were anyway. Maybe the city has revamped it?

Eh... judging by the furrowing eyebrows, I'm guessing it's all still abandoned.

Sigh.

"How far across town?" Harper asks. "No way you live in Scum."

"I..." *Think think think.* "No. Kinda on the outskirts."

Phew.

"Oh! You mean, like on Bird Street? I know a couple people over there. Which house is yours?"

Is there anyone she *doesn't* know, or at least pretend to? Damn...

"Uh, kinda around there, yeah," I lie. "Different street."

She stares at me for a long time before shrugging. "Okay. Sorry I went all twenty questions on ya."

"It's okay. But, hey, I gotta get going."

Ti opens her mouth, shuts it, opens it again and asks, "Are you homeless?"

The sun is now gone. Night is in full swing. Two diehard boys, maybe somewhere in the ballpark of seven or eight, shoot each other with plastic toy guns in the yard across the street from us. One makes very realistic *chicchicchic* sounds. A machine gun.

"What if I am?"

Instead of disgust, Ti's features soften. Damn she's good at this acting thing. "Then I can send food with you. Do you like Coke?"

I love Coke.

I refuse to eat Ti's *mother's* mac and cheese, which makes her eyes dim a bit. She soon seems to lose interest in me altogether after the refusal to eat. Which is okay with me. I remember the black squiggly things crawling around in the mac and cheese of my dream. Did Andi eat it? Good gods of ginger ale, I hope not.

Sometime after leaving Ti's house with a plastic bag containing four cans of Coke I'll never drink, I look up, only to realize I'm in Scum. The part of Hawthorn good mommies and daddies warn their kids never, ever to go. "There's bad things in Scum," a dad might rumble in his deepest, scariest voice. "Monsters that hide in the sewer and grab little kids, just like you. Monsters watching from the empty houses and factories and warehouses. Waiting because they like to eat little boys and girls. Just. Like. You."

And in turn give their children complexes that

last forever.

Scum isn't full of monsters (none that I'm aware of anyway), but it does boast some freaky looking apartment buildings, warehouses, and dead factories. I'm willing to bet there are more than a few lost souls wandering around. Ghosts. Some bad, some not. But monsters? Nah.

Hard to believe this place used to be a thriving industrial/ residential Mecca.

Long before my original body was born, some financial bomb happened and everything just simply… died. All that remains are the decaying brick and steel giants of AGO.

I barely remember our walk here. My mind, swirling with thoughts, somehow gave the unit directions and we managed not to get run over by a Mack truck or whatever. Even at this hour of night, trucks do their thing.

Ti plays a convincing human. I mean, there were times I had to remind myself that I was in the presence of a true monster. Of a thing that has existed for centuries. A creature that hates humans.

Shit, she actually looked a little hurt after I refused the "delicious" mac and cheese, took the plastic bag of sodas and left. I'm still shocked she just let me leave like that, though. I mean, she had a lot of questions. Strange ones about if I liked to draw and stuff. Then she asked where I got my tatts because they are "amazing." I whipped up lies that seemed to baffle and please her all at the same time.

After a while, though, she appeared bored with me and gave me the bag of Cokes without a word. Didn't even acknowledge my thanks. When I left, yeah, she looked all hurt about it, but there was something else there too. Something underneath that pretty facade. In the eyes. I have no doubt it was disgust and loathing.

And when I opened the fence door and glanced back, she was gone. The sliding glass door was shut and all of the lights were off. I have a feeling we weren't really in the house at all. She somehow created this elaborate kitchen and dining room out of thin air. But why? Why all the weird questions? Why all the special effects and stuff? It's like she's... filtering people. And if they don't have what she's looking for, she sends them on their way. So effin' weird.

There are only about a dozen houses in Scum. The start of some long ago residential project left to rot. These are a couple blocks northwest of the actual bump and grind industrial slum. Homes that, at one time, might have been kinda cool. Large and welcoming, but probably not very affordable to your average middle-class buyer, now hollow, dark husks. Empty windows glare like so many watchful eyes. And, yeah, I feel watched. Totally.

I won't be surprised if I find a few deranged souls haunting at least one of the places.

It's full night, the moon fat and bright in the sky, and we're moving up the walk to the first house—a massive two story, all it's siding faded nearly white—when something colorful snags our peripheral vision on the left. Caught in the skeletal remains of a bush is a sheet of paper. Not just one color, but pretty much every color of the damn rainbow. Splotches and swirls decorate every millimeter of the sheet. Thanks to the moonlight, we see these details without much trouble.

Closing in, we hear the sound of a whirring engine.

We crouch behind the bushes as a silver car blasts by. Obviously not paying attention to the speed limit. Then again, I guess I can't blame whoever it is for speeding. I know I would if I didn't know better. But Scum isn't as dangerous as people think. Creepy, yes, dangerous... not so much. There are dangers, but they're minimal by comparison to the inner city of Hawthorn.

Return my attention to the sheet of paper stuck in the dying bush. Carefully dislodge it.

Well, hell, it's not just a colorful sheet of paper, but a flyer.

I position us so the moonlight hits the flyer just right.

It reads:

TEENS ONLY!
Skin Factory, the finest in the art of body modifications, is now open!
Tattoos! Piercings! Or the more extreme!

Come see what all the action is about!
Open daily from 4:00 pm to Midnight!
Bring your friends to: 421 Willows Drive
Experience the best body art around!

Skin factory, huh? Weird. Then our eyes lower to the photo.

"No effin' way," I shout.

My girl voice echoes off the surrounding houses. I glance around, but the area still appears empty.

The person on the flyer. I know her. She's aged a little, especially in the eyes, but not much.

I *should* know her. I'd recognize that slightly cocked right eyebrow anywhere.

It's Andi. My little sister. And last I knew, Willows Drive is in *Scum*! It can't be remotely close to midnight yet, so maybe she's still at this Skin Factory thing.

And what the hell is she doing bod-mods for in the first place?

Okay, okay, one thing at a time, Chase. One damn thing at a damn time. Calm your butt-cheeks.

Flyer crumpled in hand, we set out to find my little sister.

~ 3 ~

Not far from where I found the flyer, I catch the sound of music. If that's what you want to call it. It's all wobbly. Like a record left in the sun for too long. Warped. The weirdness of it draws me to a crumbling brick building. A faded sign clings to the front of this place by a single nail (or whatever) for dear life. It says something-something, Dance Studio.

The wobbly classical music is coming from inside.

Who in the name of filthy unicorns would be ballsy enough to play that stuff, anyway? Sheesh.

I dunno. It's so weird I have to check it out. There's also a gravitational pull going on too. Like I'm being pulled to this place. Being pulled inside. Talk about weirdness. Yet, the more I realize this the more it's clear it's not me that's being pulled, but the unit. She's like totally helpless. Just going along with it. No cares. No worries. I don't even think I can stop her. Not that I want to, really. I'm beyond curious.

The doors make this freaky *reeeee* sound that sends shivers through us.

Straight ahead is a staircase. Well, all right. Going up, anyone? Why, yes, don't mind if I do.

I'm an idiot.

On the second floor landing, the wobbly music is louder. More pronounced, but still wobbly. Not classical, but opera. I think. Some lady singing all loud in a language I don't understand, anyway.

The floor is a dust blanket. Untouched. Not a single footprint. And when we move towards the wobbly music (that damn gravity thing again), the floorboards go all *creee-creee* under our feet.

A door with cracked, opaque, glass stands between us and the wobbly music. Behind the glass a shadow swoops back and forth, back and forth.

So someone *is* up here. Spirits don't cast shadows. But how did they get up here without disturbing all the dust?

So weird.

No matter how much I order the unit to grab the knob and open the door, she refuses. I'm surprised she's been letting me lead the way so far. It's not supposed to be like this. I'm supposed to be in charge all the way. Units that show any signs of independence are considered faulty and are sent to Repair. If Repair can't fix the problem the units are disposed of.

OPEN. DOOR.

Nothing.

The fear roiling through her is insane. I get it. But... damn.

OPEN. DOOR.

Her hand grips the knob, falls away.

Oh for the love of—OPEN—OPEN THE EFFIN' DOOR!

Finally, she does as she's told. The door opens to a large room with a wavy looking floor. Across this room is an old, wooden record player. The source of the wobbly music is this, and the warped vinyl record going round and round.

Swish-swish-shh-swish.

Our eyes shift from the old record player with its warped 45 to a dark figure dancing along the wavy floor.

It only takes a handful of seconds for recognition to set in.

Blink.

"Oh... shit..." I manage.

Moonlight casts its pale glow through broken windows. The figure bounds, kicks, swishes through this light, jumps into the shadows, tip-taps back into the light.

"Time," whispers the figure as it twirls by us. "It's a lovely thing."

Swish-swish.

"Constant. It's always going."

Swish-swish.

"Eventually, it reveals all. Like it has revealed you, Chase."

Crap. It knows my name.

The figure spins into the moonlight. Stops. Does this oddly beautiful curtsey. Now I see it in detail.

Death wears a pink tutu dusted with black glitter. And it wants to dance.

Its glowing, white eyes widen. "Welcome." Then it extends a black claw. "Let's dance."

Red lights blink all over the inner room I occupy. A deep hum makes the floor vibrate. From somewhere, a crazy beeping erupts.

Um, I'm guessing these are all bad things?

Judging by the unit's reactions: spiked blood pressure, chills, icky stomach, and a weird desire to dance; yeah, I'd say they're bad things. It's like all the blinking, humming and beeping is a warning system gone nutty. Probably it is.

But all this isn't the scariest part. The scariest part is the unit moving closer and closer to Death. Death with its narrow claw held out and waiting. But—jumping rhino dung—really? *No* one dances with Death. No one. Well, unless that someone wants to die. Then, by all means…

Dammit. If Death kills this unit, I'm trapped. Either inside, or cast out and damned to wander like a stupid ghost. I'll be trapped.

So I pull back on the mental reins of this girly horse. She slows, but keeps walking. This close, I can see Death's silver grin. The runner of drool on its scoop-like chin.

I yank harder. The unit stops.

"Ah," Death says. "I see you play hard to get, Chase." It spins on the toes of its talon feet. "But here we are and here we shall dance, my lovely."

WALK BACKWARDS, I order the unit.

She does, until Death stops spinning and growls, "Come, my lovely. Time awaits."

And here we go again. She walks closer towards Death.

I met it once before. Death. Not during my own parting of this world, but in the Factory. A mistake. The old angel wasn't supposed to even be there. And it hadn't been there long before Aben escorted it out personally. But, long enough for me to make a rather accurate assessment, I found out later.

Death is nuttier than peanut butter.

Totally fruitbatty.

Insane.

It doesn't do its job anymore. No more Grim Reaper-touch on the shoulder-soul taker-huge bladed thingy-point the bony finger-skeleton-stuff. Gone are the days of gathering the sick, suffering, dying. Done is the honorable thing.

Now Death toys with anyone who happens to cross its path. Even dogs.

Yep, it dances with people until they die. And just tosses the souls wherever it feels like. Sometimes forgets them completely. Like, there are no Paths in

Death's world now. No Heaven. No Hell. No After. Nothing. A good person might end up in Hell while a bad one beams to Heaven. Or a very unfortunate soul might end up in a friggin' vacuum cleaner. The Creator, of course, rights it all, sometimes, but that's not the point.

The point is: Death is insane.

Her hand reaches out for Death and I pull it back. Manage to back her away a few steps. See, Death can only dance with you if you accept its offer. At least there's a rule here. One rule.

"I promise we will have the greatest of time," Death says.

And, godammit, she reaches out for it again. I pull, but it's getting harder and harder. She *wants* to go. She *wants* to dance. A desire of the flesh, I guess. Death plucks at her nerve endings. I feel it.

Death skips around us, claw out, singing, "Yippie-dippie-doo, take my hand-baby girl-I'll show you the worrrld, woo-hoo," over and over.

She follows its creepy-ass skipping. Warms to its offer. If not for me, she'd be dancing with Death right now. If not for me, she'd be dead. Faulty unit or not, she's still a living thing. I mean, she was built, but so what? She breathes. She has a heartbeat. Her brain works just fine, when it's not altered by emotions. Emotions she shouldn't have, but does.

I try to restrain her, but my grasp slips. Little by little, Death is taking her away from me.

"Chasey-cheezy-boom," Death sings. "Let her

go, little boy—let her *goooo soon*."

"Shut up," I growl through the unit's lips.

High pitched tittering greets this. Then—

"Poor lost soul, don't know where to *goooo*."

"Dude," I erupt. "If you don't stop I'll get Bal to make you stop."

To my surprise, Death actually stops the skipping. It leans in close. Two inches from our face. Maybe.

"Ohh," it says. Voice all dry and crackly. "That ol'thing, huh? You think he has such powers?" Death lunges at us. "No!"

We stumble away, thankfully missing Death's teeth before they chomp our face off.

"Bal is nothing." Death prances around us, tutu fluttering. "I am eternal, stupid boy. I like *cookies*!"

"You like—wait, what?" The last really catches me off guard. What the hell do cookies have to do with—

"Bumble-tape! Boy! I eat you!"

Shit. RUN, I scream at the unit.

And thank the poop fairies, she listens. We run as fast as we can away from the thing.

"Dubba-do-woo! I comin'ta get *yooouuu*!"

FASTER.

And we burst out of the room, tromp down the stairs.

Not far behind, "Yippie-weee! Dance with me!"

OUTSIDE!

Then Death roars, "Stop!"

We are opening the entrance door to get the hell out of here, but the unit obeys the order. Stops. Cold. Just freezes like the friggin' Tinman. The room in her brain falls dark.

"Ohh," Death whispers in our ear. "Don't be afraid, my lovely. I promise to be gentle."

"Get the eff away from us," I shout.

"Oh, now Chase, my lovely... it's not her I want to dance with. You're lost. I found you. Come back and we'll woogie-boogie the night away."

I can resist its dark promises, but the unit can't. Death speaks to her nerve endings. Caresses them. Tugs on them. And she follows. She loves it. Like she has no choice.

Shit.

If she somehow overrides me and dances with Death, it'll have me. For whatever reasons. It'll have me forever. But—

"Why do you want me?"

A heartbeat of silence, then, "Because I am the Collector of the lost."

"I'm not lost, douchenugget."

"A Factory worker," Death says. "You escaped. You need me. Yoodie-hoo!"

"Dude, you're effin' fruitbatty."

"*Shut that false mouth of yours or I'll swallow you whole!*"

RUN, I scream at the unit. IT WANTS TO KILL YOU!

This sends icy chills through her. Like, a lot of

them. One right after another.

FOR CHRIST SAKE, GO! GO GO GO!

For a wonder, she listens and bursts through the entrance and into the night. We run. Run until a stitch claws into the unit's side. Never mind. Still we run. Run and run and run. When I can't hear Death anymore, I tell her to STOP.

Pain digging into her side, lungs burning, she slows to a stop. Her head gets all swimmy. I manage to crawl us inside an elderly Laundromat before she shuts down.

And... I'm stuck. Long enough for the fog to roll in and...

The new client's name is Sam. Her girlfriend just left and she pops a couple pills into her mouth, swallows. Maybe it's aspirin or something? She wants her face to look feline. Whiskers and all. And when I tell her it's going to take pretty much all night, if not another session tomorrow, she just giggles and waves a hand. Yeah, she's all kinds of goofy and I'm beginning to think she took something a bit stronger than aspirin. Maybe...

Fog churns and—

Sam rears. Her mouth jerks open in a loud shriek. Blood smears everywhere as she clutches at her face. Clutches? Shit, it's more like claws. Purple fingernails leave bloody grooves down her face. The girl lashes out at me. Her head whips back and forth. Her entire body quakes as her eyes roll back, revealing only the whites. Quick breaths become wheezing gasps. She makes this sick gurgling sound. Her face is somewhere between horror and joy. Instead—

"Her body is dying." From the darkest corner of the room, Aben emerges, hands clasped behind his back. "And it is your duty to dispose of the corpse."

Fog consumes everything, then…

I stand here listening to the river flows along the walls. After a while it begins to sound like whispers. Conspiring whispers.

Maybe it's not the water at all. Maybe it's demons come to drag my miserable ass to Hell, where I belong if I dump poor Sam's body into the river.

God knows I deserve it.

I haul Sam out of the chair and throw her into the river before I let the whispering get to me.

Splash.

Blink. The fog evaporates, leaving everything I am trembling. If these weird dream things are like precognitive visions, then Andi is either going to dump a dead girl named Sam in the river… or has already. Shit, I hope that's not the case. I hope all of these are just nothing. Because, damn.

The unit freaks out the moment her brain switches out of shut down to wake-up mode. Images of Death in its tutu and cold promises flutter through this room in her mind. She scrambles to her feet, starts for the door of the Laundromat, skids to a stop, glances around at the dead hulks of washing machines and dryers.

Pretty creepy, but there's nothing dangerous

here. I know this. The unit, however, refuses to listen to me on the subject. No matter how much I try to assure her it's just an old Laundromat. Nothing to fear.

It also stinks in here. Like spoiled chicken breasts turning to soup under a scorching summer sun. A dead reek. Which is possible. Maybe a rat, or raccoon, or who knows what died in here. Happens.

The stink scares her almost as much as the creepiness of this place.

"Stop being such a girl," I tell her.

This thought bursts through: *I AM A GIRL!*

Well, at least she knows what gender she is...

"Let's go," I say.

She turns to the door, but doesn't move. IT'S OUT THERE, she sends me.

"No. It didn't follow us," I say.

LIAR.

"I'm serious. It didn't."

LI-*AR*.

"I—oh for the love of granny candy—just trust me, okay?"

I HATE YOU.

Face-palm. "Really? Would you rather be destroyed? I kinda saved you, ya know."

Silence.

Yeah, that's right. I win. So—

"Let's," I send the last as an order, GO, HUN.

She takes a deep breath and steps outside. And once she realizes there's no crazy, dark figure wearing a pink tutu and prancing around, she relaxes a little. A few more scans around us, and we're moving again. I lost the flyer somewhere, but I think I remember the address okay. I think. Willard Street? Or is it Willow?

Our shoes scuff along the potholed street. The night is chilly, but not as much as it could be for spring weather in Iowa. So there's that.

We walk, keeping our sight alert for any movement or creepy stuff. There's a lost soul here and there, but they refuse to leave the buildings they inhabit. Sometimes they go fruitbatty after a while. Imagine being stuck in a place where no one can hear or see you. Unless there's one of the few people on Earth who can around. But those folks are so rare and so far between... I—

"Hey."

Like a spooked horse, the unit rears, spins, makes this loud whining noise that's pretty much embarrassing.

Our sight flicks back and forth, up and down.

I send, WHAT—

Spin, spin, round and round we go.

—ARE YOU—

Spin, spin, frantic.

—DOING?

I catch glimpses of someone standing in a narrow space between buildings as Ms. Tilt-O-Whirl does her spinning thing.

STOP!

She doesn't stop. Too freaked out. She think it's Death come to get her once and for all. She thinks she's going to die.

Another quick swipe of the person. This time they're standing on the littered sidewalk. A girl. I think. Hard to tell for sure with no real light to go by but the moon.

"Whoa... whoa," the someone says. "Easy. I'm not going to hurt you."

The unit spins, starts forward, stops. Glance up, side to side.

Sigh.

I speak through her mouth. "Had a run in with Death. I'm fruitbatty. Run away, run *away*."

We continue her freak out, when the someone says, "Ch-*Chase*?"

Wait, what? Who...

Hands snag our shoulders, stopping the unit's crazy spinning. The unit trembles under the firm grip, but doesn't try to tear away.

SHH, I send the unit. IT'S OKAY—

NONONONON—

HUN. CALM DOWN.

Then this face appears in front of us. Not what's considered a pretty face, but it is female-ish. Maybe. It's so modified by fake scales and reptilian structures, it's hard to tell for sure. The voice, though, gives the femaleness away. The yellow eyes... they look... familiar. Like behind the contacts, or whatever. Very familiar.

"Is it really you?" the lizard girl asks.

I can't stop staring at the pointy teeth. The more I stare, however, the more I see something strange. And this is also familiar.

A tiny black spot on the upper left tooth, near the gum-line. Barely see it in the dull light, but it's there. The person isn't a person at all, but a *unit*. The black dot signifies first shift placement of the teeth. The teeth I used to install.

"Who are you?" I ask, through my unit's mouth.

There's a slight hesitation from the other unit. A flicker of the eyes. A twitch at the corners of her mouth.

Then, "It's me, goob. Sara."

I'm not sure what the unit portrays, but if she mimics my reactions without me controlling her, then I'm sure there's all wide eyes and gaping mouth. Awestruck? Yeah, that's pretty close.

But it can't be Sara. Sara is in the Factory. Sara is stuck. Unless… unless…

"This is you, right? Chase?"

"I—Sara?" I manage. "How… *really*?"

She smiles. And despite the pointy teeth, I see Sara in the smile. Totally. I see *her*.

She shrugs. "Someone's gotta take care of you."

"Pshh," I say. "I'm, like, unstoppable."

She giggles and it's Sara's giggle. Right down to the tiny snort at the end. Effin' adorable, as always.

"Yeah, okay," she says.

A few ticks of silence follows. I can't stop looking

into those yellow eyes.

"So…" I say after I begin feeling a bit creepy for staring. "Why are you really here? I mean, *how*?"

My unit finally settles, realizing the other one isn't a threat. She relaxes and allows me to take full control. The result is feeling *everything*. The chill in the air is colder, for one thing.

Sara's unit sighs, lowers her head. Throws up her arms in exaggerated frustration. "I got scared, okay? I missed you. And—nevermind. Sorry. I guess I shouldn't have—"

"Stop. What do you mean 'and'?"

She blinks. "I—Chase, they were going to extinguish me. Aben, he—he came to my cell after you escaped. He… touched me. He said he'd make sure my extinguishment would be painful."

Tears cascade down the reptilian face. Thin lips tremble. She sniffles.

Somewhere not far away, someone screams. Then it's silent again. Just the sound of Sara crying remains.

"Oh," I say. "Oh, hun. I'm so sorry. It's all my fault. I shouldn't have escaped. I put you in danger and—"

"Chase," she interrupts. "I love you. Don't blame yourself for any of it."

"Yeah, but I—did you just say you *love* me?"

Sara smiles through the tears. Nods, all shy like. Cute as a baby elephant. Or, baby Komodo Dragon, if one wants to get all technical about it.

Everything else she told me before evaporates, leaving me speechless and warm inside the room I stand in. It's the first either of us have said it. Maybe we knew from the beginning, but those words were never spoken. In a way, I don't think they ever really needed to be.

Before I can respond, Sara says, "Chuck is gone."

"*What?*"

She sighs. Tears glisten her eyes. "Aben extinguished him. Called this big plant meeting and did it right in front of everyone. Chase, it was... really bad. Aben drew it out too. Took his time with it." She's crying harder now. "Poor Chuck. He was so *sweet*! He always followed the rules, but since he was your friend—"

"Aben punished him for it," I finish for her. "Made an example out of him." My rage quakes through the unit. "The son of a bitch. When I see Aben again I'm gonna kill him."

Hate roils like liquid fire through me, the room and unit. Aben has to die. No way around it. I don't know how, but there has to be a way to end that cruel monster.

Sara sniffles, falls into our arms. I hold her tight. Both units don't seem to mind. Sara has gone through a lot since I bugged out of the Factory, and the units seem to get it.

I ask, "How did you get out?"

We part some. She gazes at me through her

unit's eyes. "Bal. He said I was in danger. Had me possess this unit. I wanted a different one, but he wouldn't let me."

"How long have you been here, then?"

"Just since yesterday," she says. "Hid in that old house." She cocks a thumb at a pretty much dilapidated pile of wood behind her. "Bal said you'd be going to the house because of something he left you. A backpack."

Shit-sticks. I almost forgot about that. The money to go north, out of the city. My focus has been so wrapped up in finding Andi...

"Did you find it?" I ask.

"Yeah, but I left it alone. Thought, maybe, we can look in it together?"

I nod. Smile. Then a thought surfaces. "Have you eaten anything, yet?"

She grins. All toothy, yet utterly beautiful. "Besides a dumpster sandwich? Nope."

"Yuck. I hope it wasn't pickle loaf, or something."

"Dude," she says. "I don't even know what it was. Slimy is all I can think of right now. But do you think this unit will listen to me before gobbling down a slimy mystery sandwich? Ha! Nope. She's a dick like that."

I can't stop laughing when it erupts from the unit's mouth. It feels good. Real, honest to goodness laughter. Sara laughs too. Her unit doubles over, laughing so hard. That's my Sara. Cheese'n'rice, I missed her.

When my own laughing fit ends, I say, "Well, let me get you something *not* slimy. Sound like a plan?"

"Probs. If I don't get something real in this stomach she's liable to start eating carpet, or something."

I walk us to the dilapidated house. There's a canted hole where the doorway used to be.

"There's money in the pack. I'll use some to buy us some food."

"Awesome sauce," she says. "But… if you haven't noticed yet, um…"

I turn.

She spreads her arms out. "We're kind of… naked."

For the first time, I notice this fact. I glance away, heat building through both me and the unit.

"Crap," I manage. "Sorry. I didn't—"

"Shh. It's okay, Chase."

She might say so, but I try not to look at her when I say, "Well, I'm sure there's something in one of these houses to wear."

"Nope. I already checked. Not even useable drapes."

Roll our eyes. "Figures. Okay, maybe there's a place open with clothes in it."

"I think it's too late at night, isn't it?" She sighs. "Will you look at me, for Christ sake? You know I hate it when people don't look at me when I talk to them."

"You're um, naked, though."

She does that adorable giggle again. "So? It's not *me*. You've seen thousands of naked units. This isn't any different."

But it is. It is because it's also you.

Still, I look. The unit is well built. Well proportioned. And if not for the fake scales she'd be gorgeous. She—

I have to look away again.

Sara makes this exasperated sigh. "Okay. Fine, then. Go get me some clothes so we can friggin' talk normal. Without you being all weird."

"Sorry. Jeez," I say and go inside the old house.

It's not as bad on the inside as it is outside, and the pack is right where Bal said it'd be. Upstairs room. The room is dusty, carpet blotched with black mold, but otherwise not horrible. The only thing that bugs me about this place is the sour stench of spoiled milk. Not sure what's causing it, but damn.

The backpack is full of cash. Like, zipper busting full. Tucked in one of the side pockets is a note and a map of where I'm supposed to go.

The note is what I'd expect from Bal. Bland and to the point.

Chase, there's a bus that runs to Minneapolis. Buy a ticket and go. There will be a small black car waiting for you near the bus station there. Follow the map to the place we talked about. -B

Sara didn't follow me up here. Which is all right. Not that I mind the nakedness, but it's easier to think without her around and distracting me with it.

One hundred in twenties should cover what I need to get. Clothes and food. I zip the bag shut and go downstairs. The steps creak and groan, but hold just fine.

Sara, in her naked reptilian unit, stands just inside the canted doorway. I mostly see her silhouette, thankfully hiding the details. I can deal with that.

I grin and hold up the cash. "I'll be back, bae."

She steps aside. "Don't call me bae. I'm *not* poop. Asshat."

I chuckle. "And that's why I love you." I'm almost through the doorway when she grabs my arm.

And before I know what's happening, her lips press against mine. Well, the unit's lips, but I feel the heat just the same. Like I've been struck by lightning. Hot and electric. The entire room in my girl unit's head buzzes and hums.

She's *kissing* me. Another thing we have never done and couldn't do in the Factory. And my god of jellybeans… it's amazing.

When our lips part (I'm beginning to accept the unit and I as one) she blinks at me with yellow eyes. Smiles with those pointy teeth. Through it all, I see her. I see my Sara.

And I love her.

"Hurry back," she whispers.

"You know…" I say, making the unit grin. "You kissed a girl."

The adorable giggle. She says, "And I liked it."

I leave, heading toward the inner city of Hawthorn, reeling with emotions. The colors in my room twinkle. Beautiful. Is the unit feeling the same as me, I wonder? Seems like it. Can't really tell. Not that I care much, but it's still kind of interesting.

Andi is shoved to the back of my mind.

The Obsidious is, too.

All I care about is Sara, right now. Get her clothes. Get her food. Take care of her. Keep her safe from Aben. I know where Andi is. But, Sara needs me right now. Good doodling gods, I think I'm smitten.

With my head pretty much dozing at the wheel, I never notice the shapes emerge from the alley the moment I step into the inner city.

Not until—

There's no time to run, much less think when the five creatures surround me. Creatures I've only seen rarely at the Factory. And only then hauling away a rouge soul. Hence the reason for their rarity. Souls hardly ever go rouge, or try to escape.

They're called Raptures. Hunters of souls. Badass beings that stop at nothing to either capture or extinguish a soul. Depending on their orders. At least that's what Judith told me. I'm kind of surprised it took them so long.

"Chaaassse," one of them hisses. I'm trapped on the sidewalk before our ears really hear it.

They're tall. Like seven feet tall. The yellow light given off by the nearest street lamp reveals features I remember seeing in the Factory, and others that are completely new.

If ever there are Boogeymen, these are it.

The Rapture in front of me bends so its narrow, green eyes are level with mine. Faceless is the best way to describe them. No mouth. No nose. No ears. Just jutting cheekbones and hollowed cheeks. And, of course, the glowing, green eyes. Everywhere is all gray skin smeared with black shadows.

"Chaaassse."

The unit is too freaked to freak out. Afraid to even move, she thrusts full control into my own trembling hands. Not like I can do anything anyway. Gee, thanks girl unit. Thanks a lot. Jerk.

Icy air entombs me.

"Chaaassse—"

"Dude, you sound like a scratched CD gone stupid," I spout, and cringe. Sometimes my mouth gets ahead of my common sense. I wait for the inevitable slap, but that doesn't happen.

Instead, a slimy, gray claw tipped with ashen talons caresses my cheek. I'm in total control now. I feel everything. Wish I didn't. Talk about shudder-inducing.

"Cuunnniiing, Chaaassse," says the Rapture. "Youuu hide wellll."

I suppose it won't help any if I told this thing I forgot they even existed? Probably not. I should've known, and Bal should've warned me but... nope. I forgot. Color me duh-duh tangerine.

"Time to go Chaaassse. Aben isss waaaiting."

"Uh," I say, swallowing my fear. "No. I'm cool here, man. But thanks."

Somewhere behind me, "Idiot boy."

I begin to turn when the cold claw on my cheek tightens. "Youuu runnn, we'll killl youuu."

To my right, "Kill him now."

A weird, creepy collective sigh shudders through them.

Oh, this is lovely. Getting better and better.

Deep breaths somehow keep the thundering terror at bay. But not enough to quell the trip-hammering of my heart. In the inner room, enough lights flash and flicker to give an epileptic seizures.

I hate this.

"Then kill me, already," I say. "Get it over with."

The one eye to eye with me shakes its head back and forth slowly.

Vehicles pass every now and then, but apparently no one finds it strange a young girl is surrounded by tall, faceless monsters.

Like: "Oh, look, honey. That poor girl is surrounded by tall, faceless monsters. Pizza sound good?"

Jerks.

Not like they can do anything to help anyway,

but the distraction might give me some wiggle room. No one stops. Keep on driving like all is swell in the world. Or maybe the Raptures are doing that thing they do, to cloak or disguise themselves. Maybe, to the drivers, my captors look normal. Man, if they only knew...

"Aben wantsss youuu aliiive."

Of course he does. He wants to extinguish me himself. Slow and painful. Just like Chuck. Maybe worse.

So, now what? How the hell am I going to get away from these things?

I'm about to give up and let them take me, when a gruff voice barks, "Here now! Leave that lil'un alone!"

The Rapture cupping my cheek straightens. Towers over me. There's a bunch of shifty, creaky sounds. Like old leather rubbing against old leather. I feel more than see them moving away from me. Not much, but-maybe-just enough. The claw on my face falls away.

"Yep," the gruff voice shouts. "I'm talkin' to ya'all. Git outta here!"

The thing in front of me glares over my head at whoever is shouting. Those narrow, glowing green eyes... damn. They move away a bit more. Again, not much, but...

Here's my wiggle room. I gotta get my girly butt moving if I want to make it out of this shitmess.

I take my chances. Spin away from the one in

front of me and cut into the street. Almost get splattered by a huge truck, and sprint across the street.

A mêlée of shrieks pollute the air. A few passers-by glance around, faces taut, but no one investigates. No one even looks at the creatures on the other side of the street.

I risk a glance across the street and see them all but one focusing on me. The other one looms over an old man with a long, gray beard.

The old man sees me, waves a hand. "Run, girl! Don'stop!"

Hey, who's he calling a girl? I—oh wait…

I run as fast as the unit's legs can go without them falling off. I wonder who that old guy is? I also hope the Raptures didn't hurt him for getting in the way of their prey. I've heard stories of them killing anyone—or thing—that intervenes with their prey, but if Aben didn't put in the orders, then maybe…

The shrieks fade as I enter downtown Hawthorn, which is all lit up and alive. The mayor must think this is Manhattan, or something. Turning it into a city that never sleeps, when Hawthorn is barely larger than Cedar Rapids, seems goofy to me.

Everything appears to be open tonight. A couple tattoo shops. Restaurants. Mini and specialty grocery stores, bars (of course), and—

"Milo's Threads," I say, reading the sign above an all-glass door.

Racks of clothes line the walls. Spinner racks

dot the main floor. There's also a section for shoes. Towards the back is a long, black desk with some guy playing on his phone. Can't be older than twenty-five.

It's like walking into any clothing store. Mellow music. Smells of new linen, leather, all that. The clerk in the back glances at me, smiles, returns his attention to his phone.

Nice, I think, scanning the girl side of the store. And the prices are just right. Cheap. Must be a knock-off store. I want to buy Sara something really cool, but she doesn't need cool. She needs tough chick clothes. Something bordering practical, but not boring. I have no idea.

So, I bag her a pair of black skinny jeans, black socks, black underwear, black long sleeved shirt, and —the cherry on top—a pair of black imitation Vans.

"'Lotta black," the clerk murmurs as he rings everything up.

"Happens," I say.

He shrugs. Doesn't care. Good deal.

Total cost: $52.85

Coolbeans.

I make sure there aren't any Raptures stalking about and hurry to my next stop. A little pizzeria called, Ci.

I order two large pizzas. One pepperoni, the other a cheese, baby. Love me some good cheese pizza. Well, at least I used to. The unit's taste-buds might prove otherwise, especially after what happened with the cold leftovers from Mr. and Mrs. Big Smiles' house.

Oh well, food is food.

I also add two large bottles of water , which are only a dollar each. Then I wait for the pizzas to finish.

Total: $35.25

Who's the best shopper in all of creation?

This guy.

I sit in a nearby booth facing the door, trying to figure out what to do next. I need to talk to Andi, for one thing. Badly. Bal will hate me for doing so, but, oh well. She's my sister, for fuddley sake. Sara doesn't change that. Maybe that's his plan. Send Sara to distract me from anything else besides his orders.

I'm so twisted up in my thoughts, I hardly hear the tiny *gling* of the door.

Cool air wafts through Ci's. Again. Hardly notice, nor care.

Okay, I think. *So get Andi, then all three of us haul ass north to where Bal wants to meet-up. After—*

"You don't hide so well, Girl," a rusty voice says, busting right through my thought cloud.

"Girl… ?" I look up and freeze.

The old man runs a weathered, liver-spotted hand through his long, gray beard. He smiles. I think. Difficult to tell through all that bushiness.

"Ya'are a girl, ain't ya?"

"I—um—yeah. How'd you find me?"

He chuckles, sits in the opposite side of the booth, elbows propped on the table. He wears a grimy jean jacket lined with yellowed wool-stuff. On his head is a holey, black beanie that barely fits over the mop of grayness that's his hair. Deep lines fan from the corners of his hazel-green eyes.

Can definitely see the Hispanic in him, though not very pronounced. Guessing one parent or the other was Hispanic, the other, not so much. I can't help noticing. It's one of my things. I always pick out weird stuff like that.

He answers my question with, "No one eats here."

"Oh. I ordered two pizzas."

He laughs a bit and says, "Well, git ready for a day of dem Hershey squirts tomorrow."

"Lovely," I say, feeling stupid. Should've realized this place is sketchy, being open so late.

The large, round faced clock above the door says it's pretty much midnight.

"Tastes good, though," the old dude says. "Jus' nasty comin' out."

"Classy. So, you tracked me down to tell me that?"

The old man's tannish face droops. He sighs. "Course not, girl. Wanna know what those men wanted of ya."

For a moment, I have no clue what he's talking about. "Men... ?" Then, a mental face-palm. He means the Raptures. They must've been disguised as men to the human eye after all.

"Oh, them. I dunno. They just came at me from the alley."

The old man nods, strokes his beard. "Ah, I see. One tol'me he was a cop'n you were in trouble."

I laugh. Can't help it. It's not far from the truth, yet beyond ridiculous.

His steely eyebrows lift. "Din't think that was so funny, dear girl. Do ya have a home to go to?"

"Yeah," I say, choking down a random case of the giggles. "I'm sorry, but who are you?"

He grunts. "Name's Elm." He stands. Winces at some apparent pain or another in his back. "I live on the streets. Nice ta meet ya, girl. Be sure not to travel 'round at night, okay? There's monsters out there."

"Gotcha," I say. "Thank you, Elm."

He nods, turns and ambles out of Ci's.

Gling.

I stare at the door for a while after he leaves. I kind of like the old guy, despite his prodding questions, or whatever that was. He seems to care, which is rare these days. People caring for each other despite differences. He's genuine. And he's *homeless*. Maybe that's why. I dunno.

Unless… he came to warn me without actually saying so.

Like, if he can find me, they sure as hell can too.

Pizzas done, I begin the long, dark walk back to

Scum. Back to Sara.

The Raptures don't return. Maybe they gave up, but I doubt it. They're unstoppable hunters. Relentless. If they aren't already tracking me, they will be.

The moon casts ghostly light onto her through the window. She stands in a large room I can only assume used to be the living room of the house. In her hands is a ginormously thick book. She's only a few pages in and glances at me when I enter. All the smiles.

"The Stand," she says and shuts the book.

Blink. "I didn't know you liked Stephen King books."

That adorable giggle. "There's a lot you don't know, cutie." She jabs the book in my direction. "Like what kind of pizza I like. Bet neither of those are Canadian bacon."

Sigh. "One pepperoni and one cheese."

Sara grins. "See? *A lot* you don't know."

"Ugh. Why didn't you tell me—"

"Kidding," she blurts. "I *love* cheese pizza."

"You—okay, that's just not right."

Giggles. "Sorry, I just had to give you—"

"*I* love cheese pizza!" I turn partially away from her. "You can't hog my pizza."

Sara laughs. It's beautiful. She walks to me. Her eyes light on the Milo's bag dangling from my other hand. The unit's hand. Whatever. We are kind of one now.

"Milo's?" She looks at me. "What's *Milo's*?"

I hold the bag out to her. "See for yourself, lazy-butt."

Without hesitation, she places the book on the floor and snatches the bag from me. Opens it and peers inside. Then... she stands there. Saying nothing. Doing nothing.

"Um," I say after what feels like hours, but probably only a few seconds. "Our pizza is getting cold."

"It's so... black..." she says.

I shrug and sit with my back against a crumbly plaster wall. I open the top pizza box. Which is my beloved cheese. And for the moment, we are kind of separate again. The smell lights up every craving synapse in the unit. Saliva squirts into our mouth. I have to restrain the unit's impulse to simply devour this deliciousness.

"Guess I got the clothes wrong too?" I ask finally once the unit calms herself and we remerge as one.

Sara smiles. "Yes, and no."

I shrug again. Well, more of a twitch, really. The unit is becoming a bit unruly. Wants *all* the pizza. Guess I can't blame her.

Sara says, "I love it, Chase. Thank you."

I nod. "Welcome. Hey, you wanna eat before trying on the new threads?"

She shivers. "No. Let me get dressed first. We're all kinds of cold here." She hurries into another room beyond this one without another word.

"Well, all righty then," I whisper and chuckle.

WANT, the unit sends me.

"I know," I say to her out loud. "Soon."

NOW. HUNGRY.

SOON, I SAID.

She quiets down. Sulking, of course.

When Sara returns she's rocking the black jeans, sweater and Vans. All black, except for the white around the soles of the skate shoes. In the gloom, she's nearly invisible.

"Hey," she says. "It all fits. How'd you know the unit's size?"

"Lucky guess." I laugh, shake my head. "You gonna help me eat this pizza, or what?"

She snorts. "Well, duh." Sits beside me and steals a slice. Takes a massive chomp out of it. "Mmm."

I bet it's mmm.

"Dish ish good," Sara says around the bite of bread, sauce and cheese.

Finally, I shove some of the pizza into our mouth. Good, *hell,* this is scrumptiousness to the fifth power! What Elm said about the poo troubles the next day is the furthest thing from my mind as I chew, swallow, chomp, repeat. Drink a gulp of water. Chomp, chew, swallow.

We eat in relative silence, Sara and I.

And for this moment, life is good.

But only for a moment.

~ 4 ~

TOGETHER WE EAT ALL the cheese and most of the pepperoni. There's like four slices left.

Good god and yumminess, we're pigs.

Oh, but it feels so good to be full. Stuffed. The unit is one happy camper, let me tell ya. And for now, so am I.

"So, what are we going to do?" Sara asks after a ginormous belch. Even her belches are adorable.

"I gotta find my sister. She's here in Scum. A place called Skin Factory."

"You never told me you have a sister."

I wink at her in the gloom, knowing she can barely see it. "There's a lot you don't know, either."

"Touché." She rests her head on our shoulder.

The unit wants to doze. I let her. She needs rest. Sleep is the best medicine, or so my mom used to beat into our heads.

An unknown stretch of time passes. When I glance at Sara, she's asleep.

Sleep.

I can sleep now.

But...

The gray fog storms in. Swirling and billowing.

This one is Sam's girlfriend. Poor Sam, still floating somewhere downriver. This beautiful girl is named Amy. And she's here to bitch Sam out for ignoring her, or cheating on her with me.

But Sam isn't here. Sam is gone, and Amy, she's so beautiful. And either in hurt, or confusion, or whatever, Amy kisses me. Deep, long, and absolutely delicious. I want more. So much more. But Amy draws away before the kiss goes any further. The damage is done, though. I'm completely smitten. I

The fog consumes everything. And when it clears, Aben holds Amy in the air by her throat. She's struggling. She's kicking him. But none of this fazes him. He laughs at her. I claw at him, but he shoves me away.

"Souls are tricky things to harness," Aben says. His free long-fingered hand lifts to Amy's chest. "To hold one in your hand is the true measure of power."

Aben's hand plunges into Amy's chest.

A scream slaps me out of the fog. Another dream. Another—

"Wha-what was *that*?" Sara asks, sitting up beside me.

A real scream, not a dream-scream, then. Sara heard it, too.

"I dunno." Heart hammering. Fog fading to a dull roar in my head.

The unit doesn't want to get up, but I force her. Poor girl is exhausted, but someone is in trouble, dammit. Forget the dream for now. Someone might need help.

And... it's not even morning yet. This is like the longest night ever. Sheesh.

I'm leaving the room when Sara calls, "Where you going?"

I stop and look at her. "Sounded close. Someone might be in trouble."

"Or those Rapture things set a trap. Chase, think about it."

"I'll be okay."

She walks to me, stares into the unit's eyes. Directly at me. "You got lucky last time. If that old guy wasn't—"

"Elm. And yeah, I know. But I gotta check this out."

She sighs. "Then I'll go with."

"No." I'm thinking about her tag-along antics back at the Factory. "Stay here. I'll be right back."

She crosses her arms. Her eyes go all narrow on me.

Uh-oh.

After a few seconds, it's my turn to sigh. "Fine. Just don't be all loud about it."

And there it is, the eye-roll. Still adorable though.

We sneak into the night. I don't know what time is, but I guess somewhere around two, or three. The nowhere hours of night. Or morning. Or however you wanna think it. The moon is out in full force, so at least there's that. Better than zero light.

I think the scream came from up the street. I think. Hard to tell, but this is my best guess. And if it's nothing, well—

"You're a monster! You're—"

We pause a moment. Someone just called someone else a monster. Or they called themselves a monster. Orrrr... someone just called an empty potato chip bag a monster.

Happens.

We move closer towards this voice, and hear another one. It's low, barely audible, but... but...

There's something way too familiar about it. Scary familiar.

We hide behind a huge bush—bushes are everywhere in Scum. But the talking is done. All that remains are sniffling sounds. Crying.

I start to go around the bush, Sara grabs my arm and yanks me back. I make the unit flash wide "WTF" eyes at her. She shakes her head, holds up a hand.

Wait? *Is* that what that means?

Dammit. I wish we had telepathy or something because this sucks fuzzy donkey balls.

Sara peers through the bush, sighs, lets my arm go. She nods.

I lift an eyebrow, shrug. Conveying I have no clue what she's trying to tell me.

She does this cute little face-palm thing, nudges me, and points through the bush. I glance at the bush, then back at her. Does she want me to hide *in* the bush? Or go through it? What the—

She shoves me. Hard. I stumble away from the bush and onto the crumbling sidewalk with its candy bar wrappers, old newspapers, and broken beer bottles. If I had fallen I might gotten a few nasty cuts.

I flash her the meanest glare the unit can muster. Which, I assume isn't very mean-looking at all, because she smiles and shakes her head.

Okay. Weirdo. Whatevs.

Turn away from Sara and... see someone kneeling in the tiny parking lot of an old building with a sign that reads **SKIN FACTORY** tacked above a metal door. The place in Andi's flyer! I'm here, but—is that a leg? From this angle it looks like the kneeler has an extra leg growing out of her torso. When I move, however, I see it's another person. A very still, limp person.

I focus on the crying girl as I approach. My heart is going like a gazillion miles per hour. Any faster and the sucker is gonna burst right out of my effin' chest. Funny how I'm already claiming this body as my own. It has become less us and more me. Not sure if that's a good or bad thing, but the unit doesn't seem to mind.

Our shoes scuff loose gravel.

The girl's head jerks up. She gasps. At least I think it's a gasp. Who knows.

"Easy," I tell her. "Are you okay?"

A sniffle, then, "I'm closed 'til four in the afternoon. Sorry."

"Um, okay?" Shit. Think, think, thi—"I just wanted to make sure you're all right, and nothing fruitbatty is going on."

Her entire body stiffens. Like ram-rod straight. "Wha-what did you say?"

Clear my throat. "I just wanted to make sure you're all right."

A sniffle. "After that. Fruitbatty?"

I blink. "Oh. Yeah, I always say that when I think someone or something is—"

"Crazy," she finishes and sets something down carefully in front of her.

And when she moves there's another girl on the ground. Not moving. Owner of the leg.

"Whoa," I say. "Who—"

The girl stands, turns and—

"*Andi*?"

She gives me this deep frowny face. Corners of her mouth turned down. Her brow lowers. Then she does something that proves her identity. She licks her lower lip, then begins nibbling on it. Yep. She's my baby sister all right.

"Uh, do I know you?"

"You better," I say. "It's me. Chase."

The frowny face morphs into wide eyes and open mouth. Slack-jawed? Yeah, that feels about right, I suppose.

The picture on the flyer showed a smiling, bright, and beautiful young woman. But what stands before me now is a darker version of that pic. Rail thin, her faded fatigue jacket practically swallows her. The moonlight only reveals so much of her face. But what I can see is gaunt and sad. Her eyes are small diamonds submerged in shadow. I mean, she looks like Andi, only... older... and beyond tired and sad.

Then her mouth snaps shut. She step forward, eyes hard and glaring. "Who are you, really? Chase is *dead*! How'd you know the fruitbatty thing? Did you know him?"

"I—Andi, it's me. Really. Listen to my voice."

Her glare hardens. "Chase was a boy and sounded like a boy. You, in case you haven't noticed, are a *girl*. Look like, sound like, a *girl*. What are you, crazy?"

"I... sound like a girl?"

Andi's eyes flick to my right as Sara steps up beside me.

I face her. "Do I sound like a girl?"

Sara rolls her eyes. "Duh."

"Who the hell are you people? Jesus, what *is* this?" Andi pulls out a ginormous knife. Looks like a damn bowie knife, or something. "You tryin' to rob me?"

"*What?*" I'm a little astounded. "No. Weirdo. It's really me. *Chase.*"

She brandishes the knife at me. "You're lying. I watched him *die!*"

I hold up the unit's hands in a calm-down gesture. "I did die. well, my body did. I've been stuck in a—"

"She not going to believe you, hun," Sara says, and tries leading me away. "Let's go."

I yank out of her grip. Storm towards Andi. The knife is nothing but a chunk of steel to me right now. "Ask me something only Chase would know. Anything."

Andi's frowny face returns. She shakes her head, lowers the knife. "You're crazy. Get outta here."

"C'mon," I say. "Ask."

"Chase," Sara whispers near me. "Let her go. Come on."

"No," I say, sight leveled on my sister. "I *dare* you to ask me."

A long sigh blows out of Andi, but the hard look in her eyes never leaves when she says, "Fine. What happened to my hamster?"

For a few seconds I can't remember, but then I do. "Fluffers? He got loose and Dad stepped on him. Squished him. On purpose."

Her eyes widen, then narrow. "Were you a friend of Chase's?"

"Oh for the love of flyin' monkey turds. I. Am. Chase."

"Not possible," she says, but adds, "Here's one even a friend wouldn't know. What did Chase tell me before he died?"

The answer came right away. "Nothing. I was hit in the temple. Hard. Never woke up."

Andi gasps. The knife falls from her hand, clanks on the pavement. Her trembling hands go to her face, fall away. The slack-jawed expression is back, only bigger, if that's possible.

Around us, Scum stands dark and silent. Like it's brooding. All these empty buildings, watching, brooding. What horrors they've witnessed, I wonder? What horrible sights? I probably don't wanna know.

"It—no, you can't be," Andi says. "Chase is dead. You're a *girl*."

"Hun," Sara says. "Is there somewhere we can go to—wait, who's that?" She points at the other girl on the ground.

Andi lowers head a bit. "A friend. Who are you?"

"Oh. I'm also a friend," Sara says. "Is she... drunk?"

Andi chews on her bottom lip. Shakes her head.

I focus on the girl. She's pretty, but... there's something—

"She's dead," I say. The face. I remember the pretty Hispanic glow of it. The girl Aben killed in my dream, or whatever the hell those are. Ripped her soul right out. But... what was her name... ?

Tears glimmer in Andi's eyes. "I... I didn't kill her."

"I know." I inch closer without her noticing.

"We gotta hide *her*." Sara points at the dead girl. "And go somewhere to talk. Like right now. It's not safe to be out here in the open like this."

Good point. I crouch beside the girl. "But where do we hide her?"

"The... river," Andi whispers.

"But—"

"That's where her girlfriend is and that's where *he* wants her to go."

"Okay," I say and stand. "Who is *he*?" I want her to tell me. I want her to say his name.

Andi shakes her head. "I don't know." She looks at the body, all off in her own world. "I guess he's my boss."

My turn to frown. "Thought you owned your own shop?" Just to see what she says. Something is off here.

"I did too, but, apparently it's not really mine."

"I see." Oh, man, what has she gotten herself into? "Well, your boss, or whatever, seems like a total dickhole."

"Why do you care?"

Okay, now she's just being rude. "Because I'm your brother. You weren't this dense before..." I trail off.

Andi doesn't appear to care, which is more concerning. She says, "I have to take her to the river.

Then sleep. Yeah, sleep is good. Haven't had much. Mind is going all... weird..." Her eyes float from me to Sara. "Which explains you two. You're simply figments of my imagination."

"See," Sara snaps. "She's never going to believe us, Chase."

"That's not Chase," Andi says. Her tone is flat. Cold. Not good. Might be on the verge of some nervous breakdown. Or something else entirely.

She bends, hefts the dead girl, tries to carry her over her shoulder. Fails and nearly drops the body before lying her down. She's crying again. Andi brushes the hair from her face in irritated swipes.

"Andi," I say softly. "Don't—"

She whirls on me. "Get away from me!"

Wow... I have nothing to say to that. I wait for Sara to step in, but she doesn't. Probably just as shocked as I am.

It wasn't so much Andi's words, but the dark squiggles in her eyes. The way her entire face seemed to contract and... change. Like there's something else besides her inside.

"What's wrong with you?" I ask. My voice is but a whisper.

"Wrong with *me*? You're the nutball who claims to be my dead brother! You're *sick*!"

Sara leans close to my ear. "I think she's the one who's sick."

Andi doesn't catch this little bit, thank the god of gummy bears. Sneers at us instead.

"No," I say. "Something's way weird going on with you."

"We really need to go inside and—" But Sara never finishes. She's lifted into the air and thrown across the small parking lot. She lands in a grassy patch with an audible, "Oof."

Andi backs away, head shaking, lips pressed tightly together. She almost trips over the dead girl, but catches her balance and continues backing away.

I'm about to turn when—

"*Chaaaasse.*"

Crap.

A cold claw scuttles over the unit's shoulder. We shiver in unison. She digs herself deeper inside. Doesn't want any part of this. Can't say I blame her.

"Time to go, *Chaaaasse.*"

I slap the claw away, spin and backpedal.

Too slow.

The Rapture looms over me, no matter how fast I move away. It shifts when I shift. Moves where I move. Mimicking me? Really? What a j-hole.

"No one to save you now, boy," spits one of the others nearby.

"Well, dammit," I say. "There's never an old guy around when you need one, is there?"

Behind me, Andi says, "What—who… ?"

"Run," I shout. "I'll find you later."

"You won't know a later," another one of the Raptures cackles.

"No laaaterrr," they say in their creepy collective thing they do. Like effin' insects or something.

"Okay," I say, still backing away. "Look. I know Aben is—"

"Aben?" Andi shrieks. "*Aben?*"

There it is.

"I know Aben sent you," I continue. "But, honestly, am I really worth all the trouble? C'mon guys. It's not like I'm—"

"Siiilencccce," they hiss.

"Oh siiilencccce your pie-holes," I say. "I'm—"

BOOM.

The creature mimicking me stumbles forward green eyes wide. I side-step out of its way as it staggers around.

BOOM.

One of the other Raptures drops, writhing and squealing. The other three turn and—

"No way," I say.

The old man with the gray beard—Elm—pumps another shell in his sawed off shotgun.

"Git," Elm shouts. "Now! I'll hold'em here and —ah, ah, don'even think 'bout it." He points the shotgun at one of the Raptures advancing on him. "I got a slug in here with your name on it."

The Rapture in front of me drops to its bony knees.

BOOM.

Its head explodes into black mist. I barely avoid the goop, but I do, thank all the holy monkeys. It falls flat on its chest, then winks out of this world.

Guess they're mortal after all.

"Run, girl," Elm yells and blasts another Rapture's head off.

The count is: Two dead and gone, one injured and crawling away into the deeper shadows, and two still very alive and flanking the old man.

I can't leave him. How many shells does he have left? I dunno. Maybe one. Maybe he has more in his jacket pocket? Even if so, he's screwed. He can take out one, but without time to reload—

Cha-clack. Elm pumps the shotgun. An empty shell pops out and hits the pavement. He levels his gaze on me.

"*Go!*"

Tugging on my arm, the unit's arm—whatevs.

"Chase," Sara says. She doesn't appear hurt but —"C'm*on*." Huge tug.

I give the old man who saved my life twice a salute and a smile. A thank you.

Elm nods and backs up a few steps. He glances at the figures closing in on either side of him.

"I knew there was somethin' not right about these boys first time I saw 'em!" he bellows as I turn and run away. "Take care of yourselves, dear hearts!"

We will. Thank you Elm. Thank you.

We're a block or so away and—

BOOM.

Silence.

~ 5 ~

WE'VE BEEN FOLLOWING Andi away from the scene of Elm's last stand for a while, her maybe a block or so ahead of us, when we see her enter one of the larger buildings on the right. The closer Sara and I get, the more I can make out the sign out front.

P.R. Manufacturing.

The large glass doors, miraculously still intact, give way to a small lobby area. On the dust laden floor are boot prints leading to an archway. My sister's already out of sight.

"Andi," I call. No answer. Something's wrong with her. I can't quite figure out what yet. Just… something.

Sara gives me a look. "She's crazy. Can't you see that? We need to just go."

"Then go. I'm not leaving her. She needs me."

She sighs. "All right. Sorry."

We run to the archway. Beyond is a short hall

that runs left to right. At each end is a door. Restrooms.

"I got the women's," Sara says and darts towards the door on the left.

"Well, all righty then," I whisper and hurry to the door on the right.

Urinals line the wall like porcelain soldiers. And... it reeks in here. Not piss, although that's in there somewhere. No this is like something moldy. Rotten. Something that twists the unit's stomach in a knot of green. All topped with a hint of mint. Ew.

Broken tiles crackle under my feet. The walls— from what I can see from the moonlight shining through a small square window—are littered with cracks and festooned with cobwebs, especially in the corners. They drape over the stalls beside the rank of urinals.

Whispers bounce off the moldy tile.

"Kill them, kill them, kill—NO! I don't even know who they are! What if that girl really is— LIES! They lie. They trick you. They're going to kill you if you don't kill them first!"

Uh... what the shit is that? One of the voices is Andi's, but the other is all muddled and growly. Yet, they're like the same. Same undertones and stuff. Like Andi is talking to herself Gollum-style, or something.

Not good. At all. It means Andi might be—

"They'll sneak in here and cut your throat! They don't care. They don't love you like we do! Kill them

—WHAT ARE YOU? I can't even—Shh… shh…"

The voices are coming from one of the stalls. I creep closer, trying not step on any more broken tiles. Kinda surprised she didn't hear me come in.

"Ticks, tricks, tricks. Do not trust them—But I— if that's really your brother then why is he a girl? See? We love you, Andi. Only us—Yes."

Not good.

"But I kind of like the reptilian looking girl," Andi whispers. "She's *way* hot and—No, no, no. She's the trickiest! Can't trust her. Listen to us…"

I yank open the stall door, ignoring the fact that my kid sister has the hots for my girlfriend. Andi shrieks (at least I think it's her) and barrels into me. I toss her aside like she's nothing. Damn, this unit is crazy strong. Andi falls to her knees, stands, presses her back against the wall. Her eyes, all squiggly with black lines, jitter back and forth.

"Whoa," I say. "It's okay. I just want to talk."

Those squiggly eyes fix on me. "Talk? About how you're gonna kill me? No thanks."

She shakes her head, steps forward. Stops. "Kill you? Uh, no. I'm your brother—"

"You're not my brother!"

"Listen, I know everything is really weird right now, but you have to trust me. I'm Chase."

"Trickstrickstrickstricks," the growly voice speaks through Andi's lips. "We told you they're lying. Don't be dumb we—"Andi visibly shivers, glares at me. "Trust you? I don't even know you."

I place a hand just above our left breast. "Seriously, just let me explain everything to you. Hear me out." I take another step closer. "And don't listen to that other voice inside."

"Stop," Andi shout. "I'll hurt you if you come any closer."

Again, I hold my hands up. "Fine. Sorry. But I really don't want to hurt you. I'm here to help."

"*TRICKS*," spits the growly voice. "Lies," Andi cries. "You're going to kill me. I-I have to put Amy in the river. I have to. If I don't he'll—"

She must be talking about the dead girl in my dream, the one from the alley. "He'll what?" I move closer yet, hoping Sara stays out of here for a little bit longer.

"He-he'll take my *soul*." Tears stand in Andi's eyes, but don't fall.

I nod. "And he might, if we're talking about the same dude. Aben?"

Again, Andi visibly shivers.

An image from the dream of Aben sticking his hand into a girl's chest obliterates everything else in my mind for a split-second.

"He infected you with something," I say.

She opens her mouth, shuts it. Like she's not sure how to respond. Then, "Infected with what?" She rolls her eyes. "You know what, nevermind. I don't even know why I'm listening to you."

I tilt my head and scratch the side, hoping she recognizes the gesture.

"Stop that," she shouts.

I lower my hand. "Sorry?"

"Stop acting like my brother! Who are you? Really?"

And of course Sara picks this time to burst through the door and run to my side.

I glance at her, sigh. The girls sure knows how to make an entrance. When I look at Andi again, I say, "I *am* Chase. You really have to believe me."

"You're a *girl*, asshat!"

I shake my head. "It's a unit. A vessel. I'm inside it."

Okay, this is all too weird for her. I can tell that much by the WTF look on her face.

"I'm a soul now," I say, hoping that gets through.

"Wait... what?" She's all stares at the moment.

"Andi," I say, and just for a second I actually sound like myself. Well, my old self. How my old body used to sound. I think. "I'm Chase. I just happen to be stuck in this body." I move closer. "Will you let me explain, and stop freaking out, please?"

"*Nonononononono*—Stop—Don't listen! Lies! So many lies—"

"Trust me," I say.

"*Tricks! Lies! It's not possible! Not*—"

"Andi..."

She spins partially away, hands clapping to the sides of her head. But not before I see the blackness snake through her eyes. Even in the dull light, I see this. She screams in obvious pain.

She drops to her knees, arms wrapped around her stomach.

Whatever is inside is trying to punish her for not listening. And it's winning.

"*Shh, now,*" the growly voice says. "*Listen to us, Andi. Lisssten. They lie. They're really monsters sent by Aben's enemy to kill you.*"

Something makes a low chittering sound in my head. I hear *and* feel it.

Oh my gods of fluffy marshmallows, what's in there with her?

"*Don't fear us. We are here to help. You have to kill them if you want to live, Andi. It's the only way.*"

"Andi? Hey." I shake her. Try to snap her out of it.

"Chase. You think it's the Obsidious?" Sara.

"I... dunno. Help me with her."

"*You must kill them,*" whispers the other voice.

Sara and I help her to her feet.

Harsh whispers near my ear, "*Kill... them. Kill them. KILLKILLKILLKILLK—*"

That's it. Time to try something. Judith told me about it one day while waiting in line after work. A special thing some souls can do.

I lie down and tell Sara, "I'll be back."

"Chase, *no.* If you're going to do what I think you are, you might not—"

"I have to try. She's in trouble. If I don't—"

"—you can't save her—"

"—she'll *die*!"

I put the unit on stand-by, and leap from her to Andi.

Possessing a soulful human is way harder than possessing a unit. There are like, barriers and stuff. I break through them, but it takes a lot longer than I want it to.

"Andi," I call once inside.

The darkness flickers. Gray, black, gray.

"Can you hear me?" A faint light flickers in front of me.

"*Don't listen*, cry a bunch of voices. "*Tricks! Lies!*"

"Andi, I'm here. Can you hear me?"

"Ch-Chase?" Her voice, so distant. Weak.

"Yeah, weirdo. This is what I've been saying. It's really me. Now—"

"*Lies. Tricks. Kill him.*"

"I don't... know," Andi says. "You're dead. This isn't real. *Can't* be real."

"Oh, it's real," I say, wishing I could see her. "Trust me."

"*KILLKILLKILLK—*"

"Don't listen to that shit. They're trying eat away the good in you. The more you listen the more they feed. The stronger they get."

"They say *you're* evil!"

"Andi. It's me. True story."

"*All lies, Andi. Trust US. We are the way—*"

"They're shit," I shouts. "Listen, I think they're the Obsidious. Something Aben created, or found, or whatever. They eat out the good in souls. They're trying to kill you."

"Get out," Andi cries. "All of you! Get—"

"*We are you now, you insignificant creature. To leave means death for you. We are bonded. Forever.*"

A space of silence trails.

I say, "I need you to do as I say, okay?"

"No! Get out!"

"Listen, they're lying. They can be removed, but you have to do it."

"How the hell do I—"

"Hold on," I say. "Let me get closer. Can barely hear you."

"Closer? You're in my fucking head, dude!"

"Ah. There you are." So close she's like shouting into my ear loud.

"*Listen to us, you bag of disgusting bones! We are the only way…*"

"Anyway," I say, ignoring the wailing things in here with us. "You have to purge them. I think."

"You're not making any sense," Andi bellows.

"Don't shout at me."

"You're shouting at me, dude!"

"No I'm not!"

"Are too!"

"*NOT!*"

"TOO!"

"N—oh for the love of fuzzy potatoes, look, just try okay?"

I can tell just by her voice she wants to hit me.

"Try what?"

Sigh. "Purging the Obsidious, ye'weirdo."

"How…"

"*We can't be purged. We are forever.*"

"Yeah, yeah." I give the impression of rolling my eyes. "Yadda-yadda, forever. Got it. Andi, you have the power to do anything in here. All you have to do is tell them no and push them out."

"Oh, yeah, *so* easy." Andi says. "I don't even know where they are, asshat! It's fricken' dark… wherever I am. The bathroom?"

"With me here, you're seeing inside your body. It's dark because of them. Should be light. Anyway, you don't have to physically push them. Imagine it, I think."

I feel the smirk quiver through her. "You have no idea what you're talking about, do you?"

Damn. She knows me too well. "It's all I got, kiddo. I'm trying to help you here."

All the black recedes suddenly and light so bright it's beyond even the sun, blinds me for a few seconds.

"*Annndiiii,*" they whisper. "*You will die without us.*"

The light flickers.

"*Without us your shop will crumble. Your life will end, along with your dreams. Without us, there's only… darkness.*"

The light smears with red. Everything gets hot as Andi's rage ignites an inferno. She's always had a temper, but whoa…

"No," Andi roars. The word quakes the inner world around me. Something shrieks. I think. Not sure.

"Yes," I say. "It's working. Do it again!"

"*No!*"

More quaking. The light brightens. More agonized shrieks pollute the air. Good. Now all she has to do is—

"Push," I shout. "Push them out!"

"I-I don't know how, Chase!"

The light flickers again. Dims. They're fighting her. Whatever they are. Obsidious? Probs. The air thickens, crackles like tiny bolts of electricity.

"Focus," I tell her. "They're regaining strength."

She lets loose the loudest roar ever. Something beyond human vocal chords.

The light flickers, and they're here. Right in front of me. All silhouetted against the light. Tall, thin, black figures. All facing the light that's Andi's soul.

"*Purge us and die,*" they chant in unison.

"*PUSH,*" I scream.

And she does. It's like a silent bomb going off. An explosion of pressure that rocks me.

The figures stumble back a few steps. That's all.

Deep chuckles echo.

"Try again," I urge. "Harder."

She shoves again. Forcing everything she has at them. They stumble. Nothing more.

"I can't do this," she says. "They're too strong!"

This almost makes me laugh. The Obsidious is strong, of course, but there are stronger things out there. I have an idea, though.

"They're nothing. Pushing isn't enough. You have to *believe* you can push them out."

"Dude, why the hell didn't you say that before?"

I sigh. "Just thought of it. Jeez, give me a break here."

The light dims again.

I face the dozens of dark figures.

She shoves and the force of this one tosses me aside like I'm sheet of tracing paper. Thankfully her focus isn't on me.

They stumble, like before. Only this time they don't stop. They're blown out like dead leaves. Then...

Andi's light is pure. Clean. The blackness purged. No more tall, thin, dark figures. Wait, maybe her light isn't totally clean. There are a few grayish spots. Only takes me a moment to know it's guilt.

I stand, barely, feeling like I've been awake for ages. "Good job."

Blink. The light is replaced with Sara's new reptilian face. She's holding me, but, my vision dims. Everything seems to dip and darken. It's like falling down a long, dark well. I tumble.

Faint, Andi says, "Ch-Chase?"

And... I open my eyes to the pulsing soul of my sister.

~ 6 ~

WELL, THIS IS JUST LOVELY beans, ain't it?

Then again, I knew the risks before possessing my sister. I knew I'd get stuck. Hopefully Sara knows how to get me out, because I think I skipped depossessing class. Not that there ever was one, but still.

I've tried everything I can think of to purge myself, but nothing works. Not even force. I think she has to push me out just like she did those Obsidious assholes.

I venture closer to her. Her light. It's mostly white now. Although there are a few smudges I'm curious about. She must've been bad at some point before all this. Those are guilt marks. I think. Probably. Most likely.

Out of curiosity, I touch one, and yank my hand back with a hiss. Burns. Not hot, but cold. Cold that soaks in deep. Suddenly I feel her pain. Guilt, yes, but also sorrow. Raw and horrible. Like—

"Chase? Did this work? Hello?"

"Andi?" The sorrow fades to nothing.

Silence.

"Hey, I'm here," I shout. "Can you hear me?"

More infernal silence trails out. I'm about to yell again—

"You're uglier than I remember."

Turn, and here she is. The soul her. Apart from the light with dark smears, she's violet in color. Souls always look better than their human bodies. More, dare I say, vibrant?

She tilts her head. "How do I look?"

I snort. "All I can say is… ew."

She laughs and before I know it we're hugging. Good and strong. Until this moment, I didn't realize how much I missed her. Even if she used to be an ever-present pain in the ass.

We part. She says, "Sorry I didn't believe you."

Shrug. "Happens."

"It's so effin' crazy, you know? All of *this*. I never thought things like this exist."

"Ha. Yeah, it is all kinda fruitbatty, for sure. I've seen a lot since—well *since*. And there are things I'm still trying to wrap my noggin around."

She smiles. "So there's a Heaven?"

I want to tell her yes. I want her to believe such a good place exists, but…"If there is, I haven't seen it yet. Or Hell, for that matter. I think we're all destined for *somewhere*, but I never found out where or what it is. I was taken off my Path and tossed in the Factory before I could find out."

"The... Factory?"

Shit, we don't have time for this. I guess she should know anyway, though.

"You know that girl out there? All the tats? The one I possessed?"

"Yeah?"

"Well, I helped build her. That's what the Factory does. They build human bodies for the purpose of possession."

"You mean, like demons, right?"

"Kinda, I guess. But the Wardens aren't demons, nor are the Controllers. Neither are the other things there. I don't know what they are. Like, Aben... he's something beyond all that, I think. Something older."

Andi nods. "He said the Devil works for him."

"Probably does," I say. "Who the hell knows for sure?"

She's trying to process all of it. It's drawn all over her violet face.

"So, um, can you push me out now? Please?"

She sighs. "Yeah. Just like with those things, right?"

"I think so. Only, maybe, not so hard?"

"Okay."

She levels her gaze on me. "OUT."

The force shoves me. Hard. My vision blurs and

"Oh, thank *god*," Sara cries. "I didn't think she could do it."

I blink at her reptilian face. Tears cling to her scaly cheeks.

"Damn," I manage. Everything hurts. Ah, to be back in my good ol' trusty unit again.

Speaking of which. "Hi," I send her.

I think she smiles, but can't be sure. Well, at least she doesn't hate me still. Got kinda iffy there for awhile.

"Did it work? Is he okay?"

Andi.

"Yeah," Sara says, wiping tears. "You did it." She shoots me a steely glare. "You *are* okay, right?"

I sit. My head feels like a hundred-pound weight. Vertigo skews everything. After a few seconds, it's all good. Except... a frothy heat fills our lower abdomen. There's a gurgling sound. I remember this feeling and it's not good.

"Um..." I say and then Andi has her arms wrapped around me. A little too tight.

"Youph camph lefph me goph nowph," I say through her jacket.

She moves back. I suck in air, blow it out. Suck in. Blow out.

"Huh?"

"I said, you can let me go now. " I smile. "Couldn't breathe." The hot gurgling in my lower abdomen shifts lower. I press my lips together.

"Oh," Andi says. "Sorry, I—"

"You two gotta go," I say, grimacing. Trying to hold on to what so desperately wants to come out, I press a hand to our gut. Oh, this isn't good. Stupid Ci's Pizza. Why didn't I listen to Elm's warning? Mental face-palm. Liquid heat froths inside.

"What... ?" Sara asks, eyeing me closely. There's just enough light in here to see her weirded-out expression.

Manage to stand, hand clutching the stomach. "Just... you gotta get outta the bathroom, okay?"

They both look totally puzzled.

Sigh.

"I gotta *poop*. There, ya happy now?"

Andi snorts, shakes her head, and walks out of the bathroom. Sara, though, lingers. She's smiling.

"Finally hit ya, did it?"

Oh my god, really? She's going to stand there while my insides burn? While all the red lights in this tiny room I dwell in flash and flicker? I swear, if I shit my pants right here I'm gonna kill her.

"Uh, yeah. Can you go away now? Please? Seriously."

But, of course she doesn't. "Mine hit while you were sleeping."

"Nice. Cool." I jab a finger at the bathroom door. "Now let me..." I double over as the burning and aching reach critical levels. A groan escapes our mouth.

Sara giggles and hurries out. What a jerkface.

As quickly as I can, I maneuver the unit to one

of the old stalls. No water in the toilet bowl, but at least the seat isn't gross looking and…

"Oh thank the tp gods!"

There's an entire roll of toilet paper in the dispenser.

I get it over with.

Not sure how long after, I walk out of the restroom feeling lighter than an effin' feather. Feels great, actually.

They're waiting for me in the lobby.

Andi claps our shoulder, chuckling. The unit ruffles a bit at the contact, but it's only a ruffle. Sara just smiles and shakes her head.

A current of silence drapes between the three of us, then Andi ventures, "So… what now?"

"I say we go north like Bal wants," Sara says.

"Who's Bal?" Andi asks.

"I dunno," I tell Sara. "Maybe we should figure out what Aben wants with Andi."

"Who's Bal?"

"Really?" Sara throws up her arms, all exasperated. "Not our problem. You found her, now let's get out of here before shit gets real."

Andi waves. "Hey. Who's Bal?"

"So," I say, still facing Sara. "Say we go north. How long do you think our units will survive when Aben releases that Obsidious crap?"

"Well, maybe—"

Andi claps her hands between us. Sharp and loud. *CRACK*. Sara and I blink at her.

"Who. Is. Bal?"

I laugh. Can't help it. It's like we're kids again and she's trying to get my mom's attention. She still uses the clapping thing, I see.

When I regain my composure, I say, "Sorry. Bal is the thing that took me off my Path."

"Okay?" Andi lifts an eyebrow. "And you trust it?"

"Him," I say. "At least I think he's a him. Dunno. But, yeah. He helped me escape, so, I kinda trust him a little. Guess I remind him of his long dead son."

"Weird, don't you think?" She shakes her head. "I mean, why would he help you escape if he put you there?"

All I can do is repeat: "Because I remind him of his son. Did your ear holes get clogged? Let's get outta here."

"And go where?" Sara asks.

"Back to the shop?" Andi shrugs. "Only place I have."

And just like that, I have an idea. A weak one, but...

"*You* go back. We'll help you put the girl in the river. Then you go back and act like everything is fine. I don't want Aben to know I found you yet."

"Then what about us?" Sara asks.

"We watch," I reply.

Sara sighs, moves closer to me. "Watch for what, Chase?"

"The Utilities talked about a supplier for skin. I think Andi is that supplier."

"Wait," Andi spouts. "Me? Skin?"

"I think that's why Aben made the shop, and why it's a bod-mod shop. He *wants* altered skin."

"But why? Why—"

"Jesus Polly Palm Trees," I shout at Andi. "I dunno why, okay? Probably for the units. Real skin is always better than synthetic. The Factory makes skin, but it's totally fake looking. Shinier, or whatever. And maybe he wants it altered for a specific purpose. Like, a way to mark them. Shit, for all I know the ink you used for tats is laced with the Obsidious."

Neither Sara nor Andi say anything, so I let it drop.

"Anyway, let's get the body in the river and see what happens." I leave them in the decaying lobby.

Sara and I help Andi haul a dead girl named Amy to the river. Is this why the guilt spots litter Andi's soul? She mentioned on our way back something about Amy's girlfriend, Sam dying too. Sam overdosed on some drug and Amy was killed by Aben. Not exactly Andi's fault in either case, but she's taking it as such. All of this was in those dream-like things I was having, but didn't understand.

It's all so hard on Andi and I wish I could fix it.

Wish I could bring back the two dead girls. Wish I had tried harder to get away from Dad before his killing blow sent me on my Path. If that hadn't happened, maybe things would be different for all of us.

Instead of just dumping Amy in the river canal, we find a lower spot and sort of place her in. She drifts away on the current. Maybe she'll find Sam. Maybe this is their Path in some way or another.

Andi starts crying the moment I hug her. I whisper in her ear, "I'm happy you're okay. I love ya. Never forget that."

"Love you too," she says.

I break the hug. "Go back to the shop. When Aben comes, act like usual. However you do that. We'll be around watching things."

"What if he suspects something? He knows *everything*."

I laugh, all light and sweet. Because, GIRL BODY. Sigh.

"He doesn't know everything," I say. "He just makes it seem like he does. Pretends to be this all-knowing god thing, but he isn't. If he was, I wouldn't be here."

I hug her again and she walks back to her shop. Her *fake* shop.

I watch her go, then turn to Sara. "All right, let's find a place to crash."

~ 7 ~

Aben won't appear in the day. I'm almost positive about that. So we find an abandoned apartment building not far from Andi's shop to hole up in.

I kick a crumbling, red brick out of the way and peer through a narrow gap between wooden planks. Too dark in there to see anything. Even with the sunshine.

One of the planks is loose enough to move aside for us to go through.

Good gods and holy peanuts, it *reeks* in here. Not just your typical building rot and decay, either. Under the mold, dust, crumbling plaster and rotting wood, there's something more foul.

Steps lead to the second floor. From the outside, the second floor windows looked mostly intact. Better to keep the chill out and be warm for once. I dunno about Sara's unit, but mine... she's getting all pissy about being cold.

The stink is worse on the second floor and—

"Is that blood?" Sara asks, pointing at the floor.

Crimson footprints everywhere. One of the human variety. Big. A man? The others... well, they look a little like a...

The growl is deep and thick and scratchy. Like an old truck engine with a rusty exhaust system.

Sara grabs my arm, sucks in a breath. "The doorway," she whispers.

Yeah, I see it. On our left. Not far. Through the only open door in the hall, there's a dog. Medium sized. It bares its scarlet-stained teeth at us. The hackles rise behind its head. Its eyes, wide and wild, fix on me. The dog's ears are bobbed, weird for what looks like a mutt. And, are those spikes coming out its leg? What the—

"Hey," a man shouts from inside the apartment. "What're ya goin' on 'bout, dummy? Tryin' to git me some Z's. Damn stupid mutt."

It stops growling, glances behind it, returns its gaze to me. The eyes aren't wild now, but kinda sad. It whines.

"We gotta go," Sara whispers. "Someone's—"

"Well, now," a croaky voice says. A very tall man with thick whiskers steps around the dog. "What we got here?"

Lift my arms. "Sorry, man. Didn't know this place was occupied. We'll just—"

"N'harm done, girly. Name's Eddie." He swipes

both hands through his greasy blond hair, flattening it to his skull. A long grin spreads over his gaunt face. His eyes capture my attention most.

Black squiggles toil through them.

A fact surfaces, obliterating everything.

Eddie, whoever he was, isn't himself anymore. The Obsidious must be infecting him too.

He drags the dog back and behind him, then sort of leans in the doorway. His grin. It looks hungry. Whatever Eddie is now, he's hungry. A hunger that's never sated.

"What's your names, m'darlins?"

"We're just leaving," I say and position Sara behind me. We back up slowly. "Again, sorry for intruding."

Eddie chuckles. "Nah. Not intrudin', darling. Why don't ya come on in? Got plenty ta eat'n' plenty of room."

"No. It's okay. Really. Thanks though."

We're still backing away. I wonder how far the steps are—

A gasp. Sara's hands latch onto my shoulders,

Eddie lurches out of the doorway, eyes wide, arms extended. But that's all I see before my world is tumbling chaos. Pain spikes through me and the unit. Falling down the fucking stairs? Oh this is just

—

I end up on top of Sara at the bottom of the steps. She groans, head lolling. Eyes shut. There's a small cut near her hairline. I pat her cheeks, trying to wake her up.

"Hey," I shout into her face.

Her eyelids flutter. Open.

"What a nasty spill," Eddie says between deep chuckles.

He's already about halfway down the steps. Taking his time. Toying with us.

I roll off Sara, help her to her feet. She sways a bit, but seems all right.

"Aw," Eddie says. "Leavin' so soon? Please stay."

"No way, douchebag," I spout and shove Sara towards the planks. She squeezes through the opening without a word.

A breath of relief flows out of us and I turn to Eddie. He's on the first floor now. In his hand is a curved blade that kinda looks like a miniature scythe.

"Can't let ya leave," he growls. All of the chuckling tones vanish, as does his grin. "Pig is good, close to what I need. But human flesh... ah, now that's divine!"

"What the fuck are you?" My back is against the planks. I really need some kind of weapon because this is getting ridiculous.

Eddie snorts. The black squiggles go nuttybars in his eyes. It must affect everyone a little differently. Andi wasn't like this. Something just beneath the skin slithers across his face.

"I am nightmares," he says, voice deeper. "I am darkness."

"Eh," I say. "Nah, you're just dumb."

Eddie moves closer, lifts the curved blade. "I am… the Butcher, girly. And I hunger!"

"So, go buy an effin' cow," I sling back.

I have no clue why I'm being so cocky right now. But I think it'll work to my advantage. Jumpin' hognoses, I hope so.

He thrusts the blade at me. "You *are* the cow."

"I'm… wait, is that a fat joke?"

His upper lip curls in a snarl. "Pathetic creature. You have no idea what's coming."

"You're an idiot."

"I'm going to cut you to pieces, darlin'."

"Ohhh, I'm so scared, tardo."

"Shut up," Eddie growls.

"You first, shiteater."

He starts forward, stops. Starts forward. Stops.

What the… ?

"You having some sort of seizure, or something?" I laugh.

A roar blasts at me. My sight is all Eddie.

I duck. The blade sinks into the planks with a dull *thuck*. He roars some more. I punch him in the stomach as hard as the unit can. He doubles over, but that's all. No real damage. He yanks on the blade, but it's buried too deep in the wood. No matter how much he tries, he can't pull it free.

Ha. Loser.

I spin, wiggle through the planks and—

I'm jerked back by the hair. Hard. Eddie has the

unit's hair in his grip. Ouch. Dammit. I feel just as the unit feels. Hurts like hell too. Yep. We're becoming one. Melding together. Kind of a good thing, kinda not. If we do meld I might get stuck. And since the unit doesn't know much of anything about anything, she probably wouldn't be able to push me back out the way Andi did. There's so much about all this I still don't understand, and what a heck of an inconvenient way to learn it!

The unit wincing at a painful *riiip*, we pull away. A clump of our hair is clutched in his hand. Bastard. Pulling a girl's hair. But we're free. Time to get the hell out of here.

Sara is at my side as I make my way to the street.

Inside the building, Eddie the Butcher howls and howls, but he doesn't follow. The Obsidious may have changed him, but he's a lesser being than I at first thought. All talk, no real delivery.

"So." Sara leads me away. "Can we find another place, or you want to try his place again? Maybe he won't try to eat us this time?"

"Har-har," I say and tap the cut on her forehead.

"Ow!"

"How's that bump to the noggin treatin' ya?"

She spins and jabs a finger at my chest. "Hurts. If you hadn't kept bumping me, we wouldn't have fallen down the steps!"

"Pshh, can't prove a thing."

Sara huffs with exasperation, then lunges forward and... even as the unit is reacting with shock and I'm wondering if she's about to throw a slap... we're kissing. *Kissing?* Like, deep kissing. Like she's trying to eat me. The best part? I love it. I kiss back just as deep. Savoring and devouring all the same time. The heat of her mouth and body press against mine. It's like we're trying to consume every bit of each other. All the yearning to simply touch each other for so long is magnified sevenfold and, my god and ranch dressing, it's fantastic. My unit doesn't even seem to mind. On the contrary, my unit pretty quickly seems into it. Evidently, Sara's has no objections either.

Wow. I mean, holy guacamole. Wow.

Sara breaks the kiss just as swift as she started it. Her eyes through the yellow contacts are full and entrancing. Her lips curl in a gentle smile.

"I've been wanting to do that the first time I met you," she says, and tilts her head down slightly, chin towards her collarbone. Way cute. "I really love you, you know?"

The world around her—the buildings, potholed street—have become hazy things. All I see is her. Even through her unit's solidity. I see her. And she's all I want to see.

I lean in for another kiss but she moves away.

"We better get some rest," she says. "My unit is barely able to walk right now."

I sigh, not sure if it's me or the unit or us both.

"Yeah."

From the apartment building behind us, Eddie still howls, but he's a distant thing. A dying memory.

We eventually find a nice enough house, with moldy blankets to snuggle under.

Before I can so much as tell Sara I love her too, my unit shuts down and I know no more.

~ 8 ~

NEXT THING I DO KNOW, the sun is different.

Afternoon sometime, I think, though I'm not sure how late.

I kick off the moldy blanket. Sara curls in a U-shape, back facing me. She shivers, gropes behind her for the blanket.

"Time to wake up, my lil' Reptile Queen," I say.

She groans, curls up tighter.

"Rise'n'shine, Iguana Girl."

All the groans.

"Up and at'em Lizard Lady."

Louder groans.

"Good morning, Croc—"

"I seriously hate you right now. You annoying… *thing*." She rolls and faces me. Smiling. "Although I never thought I'd be waking up to another girl."

"Pshh. I'm all man, baby."

"Uh-huh. Better take another look in the mirror.

And trying to do your voice all deep and gruff doesn't make you Batman."

I roll away. "You can't handle this."

The adorable giggle. "Oh... I think I can manage."

Roll on top of her. With our lips probably centimeters apart, I say, "Prove it."

"K." She turns her head away, denying me. "How's that?"

I laugh. "Now you're just being a tease."

She looks back at me and I catch her gasp with a kiss. Then I nip the tip of her nose. She giggles and shoves me off.

"Told ya," I say as she gets out of bed.

"Doesn't prove a thing." She sniffs and slips into the skater shoes I bought her. "Aren't we supposed to be watching out for your sis?"

"Yep," I say and throw on my own shoes. "Let's get something to eat first. This unit is getting all kinds of grumpy."

"Mine too."

We stop and grab the backpack, but don't venture all the way into the inner city. Just to the nearest fast food joint. I spend some of Bal's cash, sling the pack over my shoulders, and wait for our food.

We eat and leave. Neither of us says much. Too busy eating.

By the time we're back in Scum, the sun is setting. A line is already forming outside of Andi's shop. She's going to be way busy tonight, by the look.

We keep walking. Basically trying not to look weird. Just passers-by minding our own business.

An idea strikes my noggin. "We need a car."

Sara shakes her head. "How the hell are we supposed to get one? Steal it?"

I grin.

"No," she says. "Are you serious—oh god you *are*."

"We'll give it back later."

"That's the dumbest idea ever."

Shrug. "Got anything better?"

"Yeah. Get Andi and run. Like we *should* do."

"And let Aben destroy everything? Let the Obsidious take over? C'mon. You saw what it did to Andi. You really want that to happen to everyone?"

"Uh, no. But what can we do, hun? Aben will extinguish us on sight. Plus he's too powerful."

"Everything has its weakness," I say, kinda in my own world.

"But what if Aben doesn't have a weakness?"

"He does. We just gotta find it."

Sara sighs. "That's impossible. You know that right?"

We're at the river now. Well, more like a canal, really. Almost the same spot we helped Andi carry out Aben's orders.

Amy, her name was Amy.

The water is dark. A black vein through this

wasted place. It whispers along the concrete as my mind drifts.

The unit asks, OKAY?

"Yeah," I say out loud.

"Huh?"

I wave a hand at Sara. "Unit asked if I was okay."

"Oh? And are you?"

"Yes and no. Trying to think about this. Like, the right way to go about it."

She takes my hand in hers. "I don't think there is a right way. Got a plan?"

Shake my head. "Not really. I get as far as stealing a car and staking out the Skin Factory, then... poof, nothing."

"I guess, if you don't want to cut and run, we'll do that. Just play it by ear, or something. Off the cuff, ya know?" Her hand squeezes mine.

I nod.

Boosting a car turns out to be easier than I thought. Especially when an old lady forgets her key in the ignition.

I have no idea what the car is. A Ford. I think. A sedan of some sort, probably. And possibly in its prime during the Clinton Administration.

In other words: OLD.

A friggin' rust trap. But it's wheels and it'll do.

I park in the bay doorway of some defunct warehouse across the street from the Skin Factory. Then... we wait.

The line outside is five times as long as it was when we walked by. Almost a block long. And it's only nine o'clock at night! Don't these kids have families? Or lives? Sheesh and rice people!

They file in, two, maybe three at a time every half hour or so.

Okay. But how is that possible? Andi is only one girl. How—

Someone else waits for them outside the exit door. It's Ti, or Harper the last time I met her. She leads people from Andi's shop to a black van idling near the curb. How did I *not* notice this before? Like she and the van just appeared out of thin air. Maybe they did.

Without pause, the customers follow her. They hop into the van without a word. What kind of fruitbattiness is this? It's like they're all good friends going to a rock concert or something.

When the van is full, it drives away. In the meantime, Ti gathers a small crowd around her. They're all laughing about gods knows what. She does a lot of goofy hand gestures. Spells, maybe?

"You seeing this?" I ask.

"Yeah," Sara says, her voice little more than a whisper.

Eventually, the van returns. Empty. No one gets out. Instead, Ti loads more in. Kinda herding them like cattle. When the van is full again, it drives away.

Somehow, I doubt it's driving them home.

The black van has a very dark purpose if Ti is

involved.

A few minutes after midnight—according to old Rust Trap's dashboard clock—the final two emerge from the Skin Factory. One has long devil horns and raised cheekbones. The other... well her mods are too minimal to notice from this far. I dunno how many the van took away, but I'm worried about Andi. A lot of people passed through there and she had to do it all herself. Either Aben has some sort of time lapse thing going on, or he gave Andi super speed powers. Wouldn't put it past him to do either.

Ti escorts the last two to the van, ushers them inside. The side door shuts. Then she climbs into the front passenger seat.

The van rolls away.

Sara nudges me. "Go."

Jumpin' lobster cakes, she's like a little kid in an ice cream shop. All kinds of eager.

"Andi, though," I say.

"She'll be fine. Now *go*."

Pretty weird she's so eager, considering we're about to follow Aben's right hand Warden into potential doom.

I put the clunky, old rust trap into drive and follow the van, which is already about three blocks ahead. Maybe a little more. Hard to tell in the effin' dark.

"You're going to lose them," Sara blurts.

"No. I won't. Sit back, will ya? Damn."

She doesn't sit back. Of course not. Sigh.

The van turns right, away from Hawthorn. Away from civilization. This far north of town turns into National Forest region really quick. And before we know it, we're flanked by trees. Mostly pine. In the dark they're looming things with long, grasping claws. In the dark, they *move*.

"Chase?"

Blink. The van's taillights are red pin-pricks. Getting way too far ahead. Wish I can turn on the headlights so I can actually see. No telling what's roaming around out here. If—

"Speed up, hun," Sara says.

"Yeah, yeah," I say. "Workin' on it." Press the accelerator down a bit more.

Don't wanna get too close, though. Headlights or not, they'll notice us if we get on their ass. Plus, I'm sure Ti has her own special soul sniffer. Like a power. Seems all Wardens have this power, or whatever the hell it is.

The taillights grow to ping-pong ball size. I set the cruise.

All this, and of course the stupid van turns onto a gravel road.

I hate that van.

I follow. Rocks plink against the undercarriage of Ol' Rust Trap. There's more squeaks going on than a room full of mice. Surprising this thing is still running, let alone in one piece.

"Where do you think they're going?" Sara leans forward some more. Any further and her face will be smooshed against the windshield.

"Grandma's house—how the hell should I know?"

"Wow."

From the corner of my eye, I watch her cross her arms. Her glare is like being poked with acid tipped ice-picks.

"Sorry," I say in a low voice. "Just frustrated."

"And I'm not? We're doing exactly what I didn't want to do."

"I know." I want to tell her it was her idea to follow Ti, but decide to keep it to myself. Probably safer that way.

We're quiet for a minute or so. The only sounds are the *plink-clink* of gravel against rusted metal. I glare at the red taillight dots ahead, hating them. The trees seem to lean closer towards us from either side of the narrow road. And given the nature of the thing in the van, I bet they really do move. I bet they really can eat you if you let them.

It's not long before the van's brake lights flash and it turns off the road about a hundred yards to our right. Then all its lights go out.

I pull over and kill the engine.

"Why so far away?" Sara asks. "We could—"

"Love," I say. "Trust me on this."

In the dark, I feel her smile. "Love? I like that."

"Total Casanova, right here."

"Uh-huh."

"Be quiet with the door when you get out. We're

walking the rest of the way."

"Fuuun," Sara says and opens her door slowly.

I do the same. Get it about halfway open and *REEEE*. Perhaps the loudest rusty hinge in the history of rusty hinges. The motherless thing.

"Shh," Sara says. Giggles quietly.

Good gods, does she think this is all some fun night at the fair? Like we're munching on cotton candy and kettle corn and slurping down gallons of slushy lemonade? I wonder if she's going fruitbatty on me. Sometimes happens if a unit isn't adequate enough to harbor a soul. Or so I've been told.

Without a word, I squeeze out and gently shut the door. It clicks, but not too loud. On the other side, Sara follows suit. Small click, that's all. Good. We meet at the front of the car. The moonlight barely cuts through the thick canopy of the trees. The trees...

I scan them, watching for movement. They don't move, yet they loom. Like if we look away they might...

"Chase?" Sara whispers.

"Yeah. Sorry. Let's go. Be quiet and... stay away from the trees."

"Trees... ?"

"Never mind. Let's go."

We walk and the woods are a silent tomb around us. I can't hear anything from Ti and the others in the van, not even a door closing. Every now and then I glance at the trees. There's something about them that draws my attention. I haven't seen them move or anything, but... I dunno. It's like they're watching us.

Okay, maybe following them here was a bad idea. Even worse idea was getting out of the car. Now we're totally exposed to whatever wants us.

Soon enough we see the moonlit glimmer of the van through the trees. Moonlight is a wonderful thing if it can get through the thick foliage. Lucky (or unlucky) for us, there's a hole to let the light in.

I stop Sara at the entrance of the driveway, or whatever it is. "They might still be close," I whisper. "Try not to step on any sticks."

"Yes Capt'n."

I roll my eyes and lead the way down the driveway thing. It's all dirt. No gravel to crunch on, thank the goober gods. Almost to the rear of the van, I spot a light not far in the distance. A flickering light. Fire? Maybe.

I point and Sara nods.

My unit draws in a breath, and we creep towards the light. I wonder if everything is going okay for Andi. Has Aben visited yet? Shit, maybe we should've stayed, just to make sure he didn't figure her out and dispose of her like we had to with Amy.

A squirmy feeling writhes under the unit's skin. A bad feeling. I should've never left Andi. But, what if that light up ahead is the answer? What if it's where the Obsidious is being readied to unleash on the world? If we can shut it all down, maybe everything will stop. Maybe Aben will give up and return to the Factory—the other Factory, the main Factory, not Andi's place. Doubtful, though. The dude is the asshats of all asshats. But I can hope, right?

There's always hope.

The light comes from a small cave cut into the wall of a steep cliff.

I inspect it a bit, just to be sure. It's clear. And it's not a cave, exactly, but a tunnel. Leading down. Torches light the way along either side.

I don't like it. Probably a trap. But then again, we've come this far, might as well see what there is to see. Unless seeing means certain death. Ha. Even then, we'd still check it out. Sara wouldn't let me leave anyway. She's too amped.

Okie-dokie, then.

I motion for her to follow me.

The tunnel's floor is crushed limestone. Limestone...

I know it's a conductor. A conduit for some afterlives. This much I gleaned from people at the Factory without meaning to glean. Stuff like that you just kind of pick up along the way. Think it's useless info until one day... boom.

We make our way further into the tunnel, the grade gradually taking us downward. My unit is all bitchy about this, but there's nothing she can do. I have the controls.

Then, voices.

The right side of the tunnel falls away for a couple feet. Like an obscure window. I yank Sara down with me before she even knows about the window opening thing in the tunnel. She shoots me a WTF look. I point up at the opening. Understanding crawls across her unit's reptilian face.

The voices are much louder here. They echo and reverberate off the limestone walls.

"This one has pimples." Ti. I'd know that purring voice anywhere. She changed it a little to play her Harper role, but not enough. "Toss him in Disposal."

Disposal. *That* doesn't sound fun.

"Yes, m'Queen." Sounds kinda like a Utility.

Wait. Queen? Ti isn't the queen of anything. She's—

"Only modifications," Ti shouts. "Other flaws are to be discarded, or cut away if possible."

A weird sigh shivers through the place.

Together, Sara and I risk a look through the opening. The scene is below us. Here we freeze. I don't know about her, but I can't look away. I can't unsee what I'm seeing. Something that'll haunt my mind forever, if I make it out of here.

Below is a huge cavern, very similar to the Motor room at the Factory. Only, instead of a giant motor, this room is dominated by a massive, glass vat. It's not the vat itself that drives an icy spike into my gut, but what's inside.

Roiling and squirming within the vat are dozens of living, skinless bodies. Their mouths gape in what must be screams, muffled by the glass. I'm grateful to whatever gods there are for not being able to hear those screams. I think, if I did hear them, insanity would take over.

They press against the glass, mouths open, lidless eyes wide. I see everything. Their muscles. Their tendons. Everything. What the hell is going on here? This is... it's... the worst. How could anyone do this to people?

Then I remember we're not dealing with humans here.

Not far from the vat of horrors, two teenage boys and a girl stand in front of Ti and a hunched creature wearing a tattered white lab coat. Ti paces back and forth. Her eyes never leave the teenagers. She stops, leans towards the girl. Then she straightens and continues pacing.

"Shall I, m'Queen?"

Ti stops. She flicks a hand at the creature. "All but the girl. Too many freckles on that one."

"Yes, m'Queen." It approaches the boys. From one of the coat's deep pockets it produces a pair of ginormous scissors.

Neither of the boys move as it comes closer, *snick-snicking* the scissors at them. I can't fully tell from here, but I think the creature is grinning. The boys remain still. Like, straight as a board still. Which is weird, because if something was coming at me with a pair of giant scissors I'd be running the eff away.

Ti must have them in a trance.

Sara nudges me and mouths the words, "We need to leave."

Shake my head. Leave? Her idea to come here, and now we've seen what's going on, she wants to leave? No. I need to find out more.

She rolls her eyes at me. Oh well. She'll deal.

The creature stops about a foot from one of the boys. It cocks its misshapen head back and forth, as if inspecting the boy, or deciding what to do.

A low hiss fills the cavern. The air turns sulfuric. Thick and cloying. Like a bunch of matches were just lit. The stink is enough to churn the unit's stomach. Saliva fills our mouth and I make her swallow it quickly. She wants to puke, but that can't happen. At least not yet.

Then—

SHNICK! The creature cuts the air directly in front of the boy. A flash of silver.

For a moment, nothing happens. The air returns to its dirt and rock cavey self. The creature steps away from the boy. Ti crosses her arms.

The the top of the boy's head splits open revealing a skull laced with red.

"Oh my… G—"

I slap a hand over Sara's mouth. She mumbles the rest into my palm. Her yellow eyes are wide, filling with tears.

Ti, and the creature with the scissors for that matter, remain oblivious to our presence. At least I hope so. Might be a ploy. Ti might really know we're here and is acting like she doesn't. Might have a trap in the works already.

Sara calms down a little and I remove my hand. She glances at me, then back at the scene below.

The creature peels the boy's skin off like it's a wetsuit. The boy doesn't scream. Doesn't move. Nothing. Actually lifts his legs to allow the creature to pull the skin suit off all the way. And... there's no blood. From here, it looks like it's congealed on the exposed muscles and tendons. Too far to really be sure.

Fun Fact: They aren't killing anyone. They're keeping the victims alive in that huge, glass vat. But why?

The creature folds the skin neatly and hands it off to Ti. She stamps it with something and tosses it in a shiny, steel cart behind her. Now, where did *that* come from? Things appear out of nowhere if Aben or Ti are involved. I keep forgetting this.

Now the creature clucks at the skinless boy. The boy turns, walks to the glass vat. Stops beside it.

Then it's the other boy's turn.

I've seen enough.

Gesture for Sara to go. Her eyes are still wide, still teary, but she goes.

When we emerge from the tunnel, the night air is cool on our sweaty skin. My unit's heart thumps hard. All of her nerves are jacked.

We're almost to the van when a soft voice says, "Ah, my beauties. Let's dance."

~ 9 ~

"WHAT *IS* IT?" SARA ASKS as the thing twirls closer towards us.

I'd know that twirl anywhere. Like that black glitter shimmering in the moonlight doesn't give it away.

"Death," I say.

It dips and turns, leaps this way and that. It moves closer, closer, jumps back. Yeah, these are the weirdest dance moves I've ever seen. It's toying with us. At least that's what it looks like.

"How do you know?"

I snort. "Met it the other day." It swoops close enough to touch, dips away. "Don't let it dance with you. Don't let in your head."

"Okay. So what do we do now?" Sara asks.

"Get outta here," I say. "Like right now."

"Oh my beauties," whispers Death. "Come. Dance with me in this divine moonlight."

The offer tugs on my unit's nerves. Pulls on her desires. She wants to go to Death. She wants to dance. Just like before.

Sara takes a few steps forward. Stops. She grunts. "Chase… I—she wants to dance."

I grab her hand and yank her back. We turn to run to the car, and Death bounds in front of us. It twirls, spins.

It says, "Such sweet beauties. Dance with me. I've come so far just to dance with you."

"Fuck off," I growl, trying to ignore my unit's attraction to the thing. I pull on Sara. We actually manage a few feet before Death is in front of us again.

I duck to the right, it follows. To the left, it follows. There's no going around it or escaping Death this time. This time, it has all this space in its favor. Dammit.

"Chase," Sara whines. "She really wants to dance. I mean, bad. I… I don't know if I can hold her much longer."

Mine too. She's really fighting now. I fight back. I try to convince her that to dance with Death means she'll die. Of course she doesn't listen. Death's spell is too strong. It overpowers reason.

"Yesss," Death says. "Come. Dance with me now."

It hurts, to hold her back. Every bit of my being is used to keep her from leaping into Death's bony arms. I can't kill Death. No being, living or otherwise can.

Sara's hand grips mine. Tight. Tighter.

"Chase," she whines. Very desperate.

I shove the unit's yearning back as far as I can. With Sara's hand still in mine, I sprint forward, dodge Death's outstretched hands, and haul ass to the car.

"You can let go now," Sara says as we reach it. "I think we're—"

Death leaps over us, onto the hood of Ol' Rust Trap.

"Son of a bitch," I say, and maneuver Sara around me.

"You can't leave," Death croons as it tap dances on the hood. *Clunk-thunk-clunk.* "Not without a daaaaance."

"You need help," I tell it. "Seriously."

It chuckles and jumps off the hood. It spins around us. Faster and faster. We're trapped in its spinning. Every time I try to dart for the driver's side door, it's there, blocking the way.

"No waaayyy ouuut," Death says.

"Chase," Sara screams.

Death circles, circles, spins. Around and around. It'd make things so much easier if I could touch it. Because, if I could punch the thing or trip it, we might be able to get out of here. If I do, though, my unit will die.

At least that's how it used to be. I don't know anymore. So much of this whole experience has proved different than I expected. Maybe the rules have changed. Maybe I never understood them in the first place. Maybe—

Eff it.

I stick out a leg. Death trips over it, falls flat on its ugly face, pink tutu flapping.

I'm not dead. Not yet. My unit's shin hurts from the impact, but that's all. So far.

So far, so good. Fine by me. I'll take it.

"Go," I cry, and we run for the car.

We're in, doors shut and locked, by the time Death gains its feet and moves towards us. Keys still in the ignition, I start the car.

Only… nope. There's this grinding *ra-REE-ra-ra* noise, but the engine doesn't turn over.

"Shit." I try again. And again.

Nothing but that annoying noise.

Sweat wets our face. Nerves are humming.

Death is at my door. It taps the glass with the tip of a bony finger.

I turn the ignition. The engine coughs to life. Throw the shifter into reverse. We surge backwards, leaving Death staring after. It's still holding its finger out. It'd be kinda funny if circumstances were different. It looks all bewildered.

When I figure we're far enough away, I turn us around and speed towards the city.

"Jesus," Sara says, her voice all breathy. "How are you still alive? You touched it. I thought—"

"Yeah, I thought so too," I say. "I took a chance.

Guess things have changed a little."

"Huh. Yeah I guess. That's totally not what I thought Death looked like."

"I heard it went insane a couple decades or so ago. Too much for it to handle, or whatever."

Sara clears her throat. "Why... dancing?"

I shrug. "Who knows why crazy things act the way they do?"

"True." She glances out the back window. "You think it'll follow us?"

"Probably."

"Great."

We reenter Hawthorn in silence. I park a block away from Andi's shop and get out. For a moment, Sara sits there. Like she's afraid to move. I open her door.

"Coming?"

She turns those yellow eyes on me. "Do you realize what we just saw? Those boys..."

I nod. "Yep. Now we know why Aben wants the bod-mods too."

Sara blinks. "We do?"

"He wants them modified because it's like a way of tracking units. At least that's my theory."

"Really?"

"No." I laugh a little. "I have no idea why he wants them modified. But he does want real human skin; that much is evident."

"Well, duh."

Sigh. "Just get outta the car, hun."

"Not until you tell me your plan."

Ugh. "Really? I don't have one now. Seeing that stuff… I'm all sorts of confused right now. Thought we'd get with Andi and talk about it."

"What's she going to add to any of *this*? She doesn't know anything about anything, Chase. Hell, she was being pretty much controlled by Obsidious."

"For the love of jelly sandwiches." I let some anger slip. "She's my baby sister and I have to look out for her. If that means including her in any plans from here on out, then so be it. If you can't deal, leave."

She stares at me for a long time then gets out of the car. She slams the door and storms to the shop.

Okay. Guess she's gonna deal. God, I love her.

I catch up to her, spin her around and kiss her. She presses her heat into me. The kiss deepens, deepens. I'm nearly lost in passion when I hear a soft, "Ahem."

I break the kiss.

Andi walks out of the shadows shaking her head.

"You two are the worst stake-out people I've ever met. Where'd you go?"

"Followed a very bad chick to a very nasty place," I say.

"Oh?" She unlocks the door, opens it. "Who's the chick?"

"Do you know a girl named Harper?"

Andi drops her keys, sweeps them up, straightens. Her eyes fix on mine. Very wide. "Yeah, I mean, kind of. I mean, I've met her."

Frown. "How do you know her?"

She glances around, visibly shivers. "Can we go inside and talk?"

"Sure. I gotta piss anyway."

Andi cocks an eyebrow. "Really?"

"Hey, just because I'm in a pieced together body doesn't mean I can't pee once in a while. Sheesh'n'rice, lady."

She shoots me a grin and we go inside, Sara in tow.

Door shut and locked, we sit on the floor after I pee in what Andi calls the "piercing room". Smells kinda like rotten bananas in here. A sick ether stink.

"So," Andi says. "What's this about Harper?"

I hold up a finger, wrinkling my nose. "One: How do you know her? Two: I think your bananas are rotting."

She gives me a WTF look. "My bananas are— what the hell are talking about?"

I wave a hand. "Never mind. How do you know Harper?"

"She invited me in her house. Really nice. Gave me mac and cheese and a couple Cokes, why?"

"Did she seem weird at all? Like, did her eyes have black squiggles in them or did they get darker? Anything like that?"

She blinks. "Yeah. Oh my gods, yes they did this

strange darkening thing every now and then. That and it felt like she was interviewing me, or something. Plus she also told me about... oh shit."

Cross my arms. "She told you about oh shit? Who's oh shit?"

Andi takes a few breaths before saying, "She told me about Aben. She set up my *meeting* with him." Her eyes fix on mine. "She's a part of all this, isn't she." Not a question.

I nod. "Her real name is Ti. She's Aben's second in command, I guess you can say. And that mac and cheese you ate, I think it was laced with Obsidious."

Andi's hands cover her face. "I'm such an idiot."

I place a hand on her shoulder. "No. You were tricked. There's a difference. They preyed on your passions and dreams. None of this is your fault."

Sara says, "We should go north now. Bal obviously has a plan if he wants us there."

"Yeah," I say. She's right. There's really nothing we can do. Except...

I stand and look at Sara. "There's just one more thing I have to do before we go."

Her fake, green scales pale a little. "No."

"Oh, yes," I say. "I can't leave them like that."

Andi glances from me to Sara, back again. "Do I even want to know?"

I smile.

I fill Andi in about the taking of skin, the glass vat, and all that horror. I tell her how she was being used. That there's a good chance the Obsidious is in everything she used to create the bod-mods here. Also used to create unique skin for units like the ones Sara and I are in.

Then I tell them my plan.

Sara's voice hits on the verge of a scream, "What the eff, Chase? Really? You do that and they'll *hunt* us. We won't be able to just slip away like we can now."

"I can't let that shit continue," I say, sounding like the hero I am not. "It's not right."

"Oh," Sara says and throws up her arms in exasperation. "I forgot you're all about doing the right thing nowadays. Too bad that's the *wrong* thing if you want us to live a little while longer!"

"What crawled up your pooper?" She's kinda pissing me off right now.

"Me?" Sara gets to her feet. "Oh, I don't know, maybe that you're frickin' *insane*? *Think*, Chase. Damn. Think what it'll do. The repercussions it'll cause." She points at Andi. "You want her dead, is that it?"

"Want her—*no*, don't be stupid. Of course not. But, look, if I go in and everything works out like I plan, we'll be so far away not even Aben can sniff us out."

"You apparently don't know him as much as you think you do," Sara says, chuckles humorlessly. "He's like an effin' *god*, dude."

Andi visibly shudders. "He's not a god. He's like a devil."

Sara rolls her eyes. "Well, same thing in my book lately."

"Faith is a fickle thing," I whisper mostly to myself, and shake my head. My girl eyes glare at Sara. "No. Listen, you have to believe in a good and an evil, otherwise this will mess you up. Remember what Judith used to say? 'Faith is a fickle thing, but it's also the strongest thing within us.' We need faith. We need belief in something beyond us if we're to keep our sanity."

Sara lets go a breath that's not quite a sigh. Nods. "Okay. Yeah. I get that. But, it doesn't change the fact that your plan is suicide."

"I can help," Andi interjects before I can say anything.

I shoot her a look. "Um, lemme think... no. You're gonna head north with Sara. I'll be right behind you. No worries."

"What about Mom?"

I blink at her. "What about her? She's at Kind Hill, right? She's safer there than anywhere."

"We can't just leave her there. I—I get this feeling like she really needs us. We need to break her out."

"What do you mean, 'feeling'?" I hope it's not what I think it means.

"I don't know. Just this strong feeling like we NEED to go there."

I hope I convey my dubious expression enough. "A feeling... like a voice?"

Her eyes widen. "Oh it's not a voice. Like I said, it's a feeling. We need to go there. We need to bring Mom with us."

All I can do is stare at her as she plays with a silver stud on the tray next to the piercing chair.

Tears trickle down her cheeks. "She needs us. Can't you feel it? She's our mom."

"I know," I say and sigh. "But how are you gonna get in? Last I knew they have a huge gate and guards and security up the red ass of a baboon there."

She stands and flaps her arms up and down. "I don't *know*. I just have to go to her. I feel it. This sort of pull. Don't you?"

Now that she draws attention to it. I look away. "Yeah. Not like a strong pull, but yeah, I feel it."

"She's just as crazy as you are," Sara says. "Jesus, are you two hearing yourselves? Chase, I get your plan and all, and you might be able to get away without getting your ass extinguished. *Might*. But... Andi... there's no way we can get to your mom if it's as guarded as Chase says."

Uh-oh.

"Up yours," Andi spits.

Sara's mouth opens a little. Her eyes get all big. She looks genuinely hurt. Dammit...

"Whoa," I say. I make sure Andi sees my glare. "That was uncalled for, ye weirdo."

"I don't care," she growls. "She has no right at all to tell me what to do."

"She's a part of this, and I love her."

Sara's gape shifts from Andi to me. Heat rises to my cheeks. Great, I'm probs blushing.

"I get that," Andi says. "But damn. I *have* to do this. I have to see."

I nod. "Then you'll have to wait for me to do my thing."

"Chase," Sara says. "If you do what you're going to do, we won't have time to break your mom out."

I shrug. "Probably not. But it's something we have to try. Andi, what was Mom like before they committed her?"

She shakes her head. Might hurt to think about. Probably. "Crazy. How else? After Dad killed you, after he was sent to prison, she was all right for a while. I mean, she cried a lot, but eventually she stopped and I thought she was getting better. We hung out a lot. Played video games. Went on hikes. She started laughing and smiling again. Then... one night I woke up to her screaming." She fetches a breath. So many tears cascade down her face. "Chase, she was in the closet. And when I opened the door she almost shot me with Dad's pistol. Like, she actually fired. Felt the bullet go right by my face. When she realized it was me, she dropped the gun and cried. She kept saying she was sorry over and over. Said she thought I was *him*. I asked who the hell she was talking about and she said, 'The Devil'."

My mouth opens, shuts. I have no idea what to

say. Andi continues.

"She said the Devil was trying to give her his babies. Said he promised her the universe. From then on, she wasn't the same. Day after day she got weirder and weirder. Once she even wrapped me in aluminum foil to protect me from what she called 'the Devil's parasites.' She missed a lot of work. Got fired. Our water and electricity got shut off. It wasn't until her friend Shanna stopped by when things turned from weird as shit to effin' *scary*."

I wait, still speechless. I gesture for her to go on.

"I was in my room drawing up ideas for a cool bod-mod. Heard Mom and her talking. I figured maybe Shanna could talk Mom out of her craziness so I kind of tuned them out. That's when I heard the gunshot. Then... screaming. When I ran into the living room it wasn't Shanna who was screaming. Mom was. Shanna was on the floor. Blood covered the front top half of her white blouse. She didn't move. Mom was on her knees jabbing the gun's barrel at Shanna's face and screaming. She said a bunch of gibberish, but a few words I understood. Stuff like, 'Demon,' 'false messenger,' 'Devil's concubine.' Anyway, our neighbor, Mr. Veny—you remember him, Chase, I'm sure—heard the gunshot and came to see if everything was okay. He called the cops and while all that was happening I packed some stuff and split. Not far at first. I stayed close by, long enough for them to commit her to Kind Hill, and I knew they'd stick me in foster care or something. So I ran."

After a minute or two, I manage, "Wow."

"Right," she says.

"If your mom is that crazy," Sara says, "then why try to break her out and take her with? She'd try to kill us all, I bet."

"Don't you see," I say, voice low. "It was Aben all along. For some reason he targeted our mom too. He was trying to impregnate her, or something. Drove her fruitbatty."

"You don't know that," Sara spouts. "People go crazy all the time without warning or reason."

"True. But what if I'm right and that's why she did what she did? What if now she's okay?"

"If she's still in the asylum, she's obviously not okay."

"Think what you want. We're going."

Sara, giving up, nods. "Fine. That's if you make it back from your little seek and destroy mission. And did you forget about Death? It's still out there!"

"If I don't come back, go on without me."

Neither Sara nor Andi say anything. I know too well that if I don't return they'll part ways. Alone. Sara will take the backpack of cash and go north while Andi will more than likely try to break Mom out of Kind Hill by herself, and get arrested because of it. Foster care would be the least of her worries then.

"Anyway," I say, and start towards the door. "I'd

suggest getting away from here. Meet at the old mill by Kind Hill."

"Chase," Sara says, and walks over to me.

I take her in my arms. Our kiss is something only a romance author could describe with any accuracy. It's long and slow and passionate. Beautiful, actually.

When our lips part, Sara whispers, "Be careful. I love you."

I nod, blow Andi a kiss, and leave.

The night air is full of chills and I wonder if I'll ever see either of them again.

~ 10 ~

DOESN'T TAKE ME LONG to drive back to the real Skin Factory, not the bod-mod shop but the place in the woods. I park in the same spot as before.

Death is nowhere to be seen, thank the pink floundernuts of purgatory. At least, so far. I hope it finally gave up and moved on to some other prey. If not, oh well, I'm here now and there's no turning back.

Outside the tunnel, silence. But the van is still here, and the torches are still lit, so someone must still be here. I enter, avoiding any loose rocks or gravel. I crouch under the opening, draw in a breath, rise up, and peek down just in time to see the creature with the tattered lab coat yank off another person's skin.

Our breath whooshes out like the unit has been slugged in the gut. It's the *whatever* expression on the creature that's probably the worst. I mean, peeling people's skin off is horrible. But… that expression of nothing is as unnerving as shit.

I don't see Ti. Instead of handing her the skin, the creature slaps it into the claws of a Utility, which folds the skin, plops it into the steel cart, and waits for the next. Looks totally bored, the ugly fucker.

So, where the shit is *Ti*? If she's wandering the tunnels, I might be screwed.

Standing in front of the creature with the lab coat and giant scissors are six teenagers. All with different bod-mods and tattoos, and piercings. In the glass vat, the open-mouthed, wide eyed skinless continue to writhe.

A chill shivers through both me and the unit.

Yeah, I gotta stop this.

Time to do what I came here to do.

As I creep onward, the tunnel gradually descends, a casual slope into what might as well be a section of Hell. As I navigate the unit, her nerves ignite and blink around me. She's scared. Her stomach hurts. She wants to leave. And as we move further on, the air gets colder and colder. This is like a trigger for the rest of her senses. It sparks the fear, ushers on the sick feeling.

I come to an intersection. Glance left, then right. Both appear empty. I take the tunnel on the left, descending further. At another intersection, I hear the echoes of Utility gibberish, and the growling grunts of the creature in the lab coat.

"How'many, Cutter?" asks the Utility.

"Many," growls the creature called Cutter.

Fitting...

"Ah."

Turn right this time. In front me the tunnel opens up into a massive cavern.

I'm here.

I swallow down a lump in the unit's throat. Try to settle her stomach. This takes a bit of effort, but the sick feeling soon passes.

Directly ahead, the Utility comes into view. It folds another skin suit, places it in the cart. I cling to the shadows of the wall. I came here with no weapon, which is dumb. Why didn't I at least pick up a strong stick outside? Good bumblebee balls, really? What the hell was I thinking?

Oh, wait, I wasn't. As usual.

My sight happens on a softball sized rock. Eh, what am I supposed to do with that? I mean, I can bash one of them in the head, but then what? The other will have me in its clutches before I have time to turn around. If I can find two rocks I can charge in and throw one at each of the creatures. If I'm lucky I'll hit both in the head hard enough to knock them out. But what if I miss?

Dammit.

I stare at the nearest torch. Watch the flames dance and lick the thick air of the cavern. My eyes trace over the stick part of the torch. Down... down. It's about three feet long. The other end has been whittled down to a point. Not like a sharp point. Kinda blunt. But maybe...

Slowly, an idea forms.

I pick up the rock and slip the torch out of its holder. The weight of the torch feels good in the unit's hand. She doesn't like my new idea. Not at all. But what other choices do we have? It's either this or leave. Leave these poor people here to suffer. Let the skinning and horror show continue.

I can't do that.

Pause on the verge of the attack. How the hell am I supposed put their skin back on?

Eff it.

I charge.

The Utility whirls toward me, all surprised eyes and gaping maw, before I bash that ugly face in with the rock. It drops, body twitching, blood oozing.

The Cutter manages a shriek before I jam the lit end of the torch into its crooked mouth. The flames go out with a *pssft*. Smoke billowing, the Cutter stumbles back. It gags, claws at its throat. I yank the torch out, flip it around and press the pointy end at the creature's throat. It drops to its knees, claws up and shaking. It's giving up whatever fight it had. The scissors clink on the stone floor. I pick them up with my free hand.

"Tell me," I whisper. "Can you put their skin back on?" I nod at the vat of the skinless.

The Cutter makes this weird clucking sound, but doesn't answer my question. I press the tip of the torch harder into its throat. Brandish the scissors.

"Do you wanna know what it feels like?" I

SHNICK the scissors for effect. "Cause I can totally make that happen if you don't answer me right now. Can you put their skin back on?"

It clucks a couple of times then…

"Y-yes," it gurgles.

"Good. Let's—"

"Not all skins here, though," it spouts. "M'Queen take to Factory."

So that's where Ti is. Good.

"Well let's get done what we can," I say. I nod at the vat. "Will they be in pain if I let them out of there?"

"N-no. Numb. Jus'scared."

"Okay. Get up. Let them out. Then you're going to put the skin back on whoever you can."

It nods and stands. I prod it to the vat doors.

"M'Queen'll kill you," the Cutter growls.

"Uh-huh. Hurry up, ugly."

It unlocks the doors and, ah hell, they all pour out. Their screams of utter horror are enough to drive anyone mad. I turn down the hearing of my unit to sort of muffle the worst of it. They run towards the tunnel I just came from.

"Wait," I shout. "I'm here to help! We can put your skin back on!"

Muffled chuckles draw my attention back to the Cutter.

"They gone mad. No help for'em."

I watch the last of them disappear down the tunnel and grit my teeth. I turn to the Cutter.

"You son of a bitch."

It chuckles. "Ya didn't ask what they be like. Jus'get'em out."

All of the skinless teenagers are gone, leaving just the Cutter and I here. Rage I've never really felt before surges out of me, swirls inside the unit, blasts to the arm holding the pointed end of the torch to the monster's throat.

The wooden tip bursts from the back of the Cutter's neck before I have time to stop it. Black blood spurts out of its mouth, bubbling and frothing as it gags and wrenches away from me. I watch, stunned, as it lurches towards a door I hadn't noticed before, beyond the cart.

One. Two steps. Three. Fou—

It face-plants on the floor next to the motionless Utility. Its body quivers, then falls still. A pool of blood spreads around it.

Adrenaline like effin' fire burns everything inside the unit. She wants to run. Just run and run and run. I keep her still, though our body jitters with the urge to flee.

I turn to the vat. It needs to be destroyed. Somehow. I hold up the scissors and inspect them. The tool has powers. Otherwise, it'd actually have to make contact with the skin to cut it off. The Cutter never touched anyone with them. Just *SNICKED*.

Shrug. Worth a shot.

I walk up to the vat and... *SHNICK*.

Nothing happens.

Not right away, anyway.

A few seconds later, a shrill squeal sounds. The vat vibrates. A heavy thrum that shakes the floor and trembles through us.

Then the doors pop off their hinges and *flump* on the stone. They don't break, but a simple glance at the hinges tells me there will be no fixing them unless replaced. They've been cut cleanly through.

Nice.

That's all the damage the scissors will make, though. I try snicking them in front of the glass and nothing happens. At all. Not even the vibrating thing.

Well shit.

I stow the scissors in the back pocket of our jeans and run towards the tunnel. Better get out before—

A sudden epiphany strikes.

I hurry to the cart. Maybe I can convince a few of them to put their skin back on. I have no damn idea how to do it, but who knows. Might figure it out.

Pushing the cart out of the tunnels and into the dim light of dawn, I don't even see what's waiting for me at the car until it's too late.

Ti detaches herself from the hood and says, "Well now, if it isn't number 51Z-60…"

Without her Harper mask on, she's just a beautiful woman. Maybe in her middle twenties.

"Chase," I say.

She grins. "Oh, that's right. You're still clinging to this life. Too bad it has come to an end."

"Pfft. Your slip is showing."

"Foolish boy," she hisses. "Such a foolish boy you are. He's coming to see to you himself, you know? He is not happy, I assure you."

"Hey I got a question for you," I blurt. Not caring. "If you're so high and mighty, how come you didn't know it was me when you were playing Harper?"

The grin droops a bit, but she doesn't answer the question. Instead, "Your death is going to be long and slow, with as much pain as Aben can inflict before you finally extinguish."

"Yeah, yeah, something about death and pain. You probably better go check on your Cutter back there. He had a slight... accident."

The grin vanishes. "What did you do?"

My turn to grin. "Thought you things knew everything. We'll just call this a slip—"

Her hand wraps around our throat before I can finish. It clamps down. Hard. Alligator hard. Then we can't breathe.

"What. Did. You. Do?" Spittle sprays into our face with every word.

Pretty gross.

I can't reply, of course. She's choking us. All that comes out are gurgling sounds.

"You weak, pathetic creature," she growls. Gone is the girly voice. She's showing me her true self now. The monster behind the mask. Darkness snakes under her skin. "When Aben finds out about this he will make you pay. He will—"

"*Ahhhhh.*" The approaching voice is barely above a whisper.

Ti blinks. Her hand loosens enough for us to slip out of her grip. We fall to our knees as the unit coughs and gags. I help her regulate her breathing. I take full control and roll us away from Ti. As we gain our feet, about to run, Death bounds out of the ditch and spins on the tips of its broken slippers.

Behind me, Ti roars, "This does *not* concern *you!* Be gone!"

With light titters, Death dips and turns, twirls around. It doesn't even glance my way.

"Ah, now, *Tiiii*," it croons. "Come dance with m*eeee.*"

"You're interrupting Factory business, you mad idiot."

"Yesss."

I listen to the scrape-crunch as Death dances. I start forward, but—

"Do not move, Chase," Ti shouts. "Aben—"

"Shh," Death says. Its voice is soft, caressing. So much so the unit feels that alluring tug again.

"This is *not* a... a... what are you doing?" Ti's voice wavers over the place. Deep and low, high and shrill, somewhere in between.

I sever the unit's paralysis and run. She pleads for me to go back but, um... no. I did what I came here to do, well, more or less. Time to bug out before Aben gets here.

I get in the car, start it (thank the mighty gods it starts without complaints), and do a three point turn. As the headlights flash across the road, I see something I never thought would be possible.

Ti swings in Death's embrace as it does this weird waltz-ish dance. Her head lolls from side to side, bonelessly. Her eyes are wide, completely black, arms dangling and swishing with every turn Death makes. In this brief glimpse I see Death and its work. I see a dead Warden. A being once thought to be impervious to death, or more rightly so, Death.

Before the light passes, Death's mouth opens. Its lower jaw unhinges like a snake. Before the light passes, most of Ti's head is in Death's gaping maw.

An icy shiver prickles through the unit, then we're speeding away. I press the accelerator to the floor and watch the speedometer hit eighty miles per hour. I manage to slow to thirty to make the right turn and head back to Hawthorn.

Eating her, I think. *Death was really eating her.*

Aben is going to be one pissed off... well... whatever the hell he is.

Instead of heading directly into Hawthorn, I use back roads to circle it and come in from a different direction.

Hope Sara and Andi made it to the mill all right.

Jumping Jesus Goose Eggs, I hope they're okay.

KIND HILL

~ 1 ~

SARA PRACTICALLY JUMPS into my arms, slathering me with kisses, the moment I arrive at the mill.

When we part, I give Andi a strong hug and look at both of them. I'm beat. But there's still a lot to do.

I imagine my girl eyes are huge with urgency, when I say, "We gotta hurry."

"Did you do it?" Sara asks.

"I let all of them go, but they were... fruitbatty. Didn't even care to get their skins back. Ran away. Didn't even see one on my way here." I sigh. "And Death got Ti."

Sara opens her mouth, shuts it. A weird "huh" sound escapes. That's all.

"Right," I say. "I didn't think she could ·die either, but..."

"Aben's gonna be pissed, isn't he?" Andi spouts.

"Shit yeah he will. Ti was his right hand... well,

his right hand whatever she was."

"We…" Sara manages. "Chase… we really have to go. Like, yesterday."

"I know. C'mon, let's get Mom and skip town."

"You still want to get her after all *that*?" Sara's voice is near cracking.

"She's our *mom*," Andi spits.

"I know that," Sara says. "I know! And I get it. But if Aben finds us before we get her out, we're, sorry, but we're screwed."

Andi flips her off, spins, and storms away in the direction of Kind Hill Asylum.

"Andi," I yell, not that far behind her. "Hey. Wait up!"

She doesn't slow down. Ugh.

She's starting up the hill to the asylum when I finally catch up.

"What's your deal, lady?" I huff.

She cocks a thumb over her shoulder. "What do *you* think."

"She's just scared, ye weirdo. No need to be a jerknut about it."

"Whatever."

I grab her arm and spin her to me. "Look. She's amazing. You're amazing. I love you both and I will not have you hating each other over this. We need to work together, dammit." I let her go and step away. "We *are* going to try and get Mom out. I promised. But if we can't, we can't, okay?"

"Fine," she says. There's bit of venom in her

tone.

Sara steps next to me, crosses her arms and glares at Andi. "You done?"

Andi rolls her eyes and continues up the hill. By her expression, I'm sure she wouldn't mind if Sara fell down a well somewhere.

We come to a deep ditch. Beyond this is a narrow, paved road. And beyond that lie the gates to Kind Hill Asylum. We gather in the ditch, crawling on our stomachs so we can peek street level across the road to the asylum. Just enough so the tops of our heads show.

The gates are shut, of course. Behind them stands a small house. I can make out the shadow of a person pass by one of the tiny windows.

"Must be where the guards hang out," I whisper.

The gates are really high and topped with razor wire. At the same height, the walls extend on either side. Thick, cement walls. Also topped with razor wire. There aren't any trees, or anything close enough to aid us in any attempt to get over.

Lovely.

We scoot back down the embankment and sort of just stare at each other. Sara shakes her head at me. I nod. She's trying to tell me it's not worth the risk. Ah, but what if it is?

She shrugs. I sigh. She—

"Oh for the love," Andi rasps. "Will you two knock it off and tell me what's going on?"

I clear my throat. "Sorry. Looks pretty bleak."

"Well it's not supposed to be easy, right?"

"Stop," I say. "Getting pissy isn't gonna help us. Can you think of any way in? Maybe a tree, or…"

"Trees aren't close enough," Andi says, then sighs. "There has to be a way. Everything has a—"

"Weakness," I finish for her. I thought the same thing at the Factory.

"Yeah."

"We better think of something soon," Sara says. She faces me. "I know how important this is to both of you, and I'm here to help in any way I can. But if we can't even get in…"

She lets it hang there in the air. Yeah, I get it. Don't like it, but I get it.

I suck in a breath, glance around. After a few more seconds a grin spreads along my girly, tatted face.

A little proverbial light bulb flickers. Probs not a good thing, but…

I tell them my idea.

"Wait, what?" Sara blurts. Thankfully not too loud.

"It's the only way I can see, baby," I say.

"You think it'll work?" Andi shifts from one elbow to the other. "Like, really?"

"Ha. If I knew for sure, it wouldn't be such a fruitbatty plan, would it?"

She nods. "You belong in there anyway." She smiles.

"Pshh, stop being jelly and watch me work."

Before either Sara or Andi can hogtie me, I scramble out of the ditch and shuffle across the road.

When I cross the center line, I let loose the loudest scream this unit's lungs can produce. Which doesn't disappoint.

I jitter and shuffle. I scream, mumble a bunch of stuff, scream. My arms flail, fall to my sides, flail some more. I force my head to twitch from side to side.

I make it about ten feet from the gate when two guards dressed in all black uniforms burst from the guard shack. They run to the gate. One is younger, maybe middle twenties and scrawny. The other is chubby, middle aged, or close to that. The younger one has a gun drawn.

"Stop," shouts the middle-aged guard.

I don't stop. I twitch and jitter and shriek, and continue towards the gates. The younger guard has the gun aimed right at me.

"Open the gates." A booming voice shakes the air from the direction of the guard house. "Hannon sees her in the cameras and wishes to admit her!"

Then a third guard, this one much older than Middle-Aged, strides to the gates. His hair is short and gray. His face—from what I can tell—is wrinkled yet has a chiseled look to it. He's trim, broad shouldered. Kinda scary. He places a hand over the top of the younger guard's gun and lowers it.

"You open the gates, Mike," says the old guard.

The young guard, Mike, holsters his gun and runs to the small house.

Meanwhile, I drop to my knees and howl. I claw at the air and shout, "They're coming! Coming, coming! They're coming!"

The old guard whispers something I can't quite hear to Middle-Aged. Middle-Aged nods.

A shrill squeak pierces the early morning. Then, a grinding as the gates slowly open. Middle-Aged moves out, helps me to my feet and ushers me onto the asylum's grounds. I just hope Sara and Andi remember what to do next as the guards lead me towards the shack.

Mike opens the house door. His face is all wide eyes. "Damn, Cap, she looks—"

"Are ya dumb or do ya belong in there?" Cap, the old guard, points at the huge castle-like building ahead.

"I... huh?"

Cap smacks his forehead. "Shut the goddamn gates, Mike."

"Oh... *oh*! Okay, sorry." Mike disappears back into the house and the gates squeak shut. A loud, metallic *CLINK* signals them being locked.

Cap sighs, faces Middle-Aged. "Where'd ya find him again? Local simple-minded bar, or something?"

Middle-Aged snorts. "HPD. Used to be a good cop, but—"

Cap waves a hand. "Yeah-yeah, but he couldn't handle the homicides anymore. Got it. He gets back out, I want you and him to escort this beauty to Hannon. Room 216."

"Yes sir." Middle-Aged frowns. "But I thought he sends out orderlies for that?"

Cap shrugs. "Must think this one is special."

Middle-Aged nods and says no more.

Not sure if Sara and Andi made it inside, though. I'll just have to play my part until I know for sure. Which I'm doing. I twitch and mumble shit all over the place and they're totally buying it. Damn... I should've been an actor.

Mike rushes out of the guard house.

"Mike, I want you and Gary here to escort this girl to Hannon in Room 216," Cap says in his deep, booming voice.

Mike nods, latches onto my free arm. Maybe a little too tight, but I'll deal. The two guards lead me up a flagstone path towards the asylum.

The sun's heat is already baking into me. The birds sing their songs. Other than what's going on here, today is just your average summer day in Iowa. The guards' boots *thuck-thuck* on the flagstones. I realize I've slacked a bit on my acting. Bring back the twitches and jitters and mutterings. Pretend to struggle in their grips.

"Shh, now," Gary says. "You'll be all right."

"Hey, Gary," Mike says.

"Yeah?"

"Since when does Hannon have us escort patients to room 216?"

"Since Cap got the orders from Hannon himself. I don't know, kid. Just go with it."

We mount the concrete steps leading to the asylum's front doors. Huge doors that look like they're made of iron. Probably are. This place is an effin' fortress. Note to self: In case of zombie apocalypse, GO HERE.

The doors open. Two huge guys wait on the other side of the threshold. Like, broad and tall huge. But it's not their bodies that draws my total attention. Black lines squiggle in their eyes.

Uh-oh.

"Hannon waits," one of the huge men says. His voice is slow, monotone, kinda creepy.

"You guys taking it from here?" Gary asks.

"Yes."

The guards pass me to the two huge dudes. Their grips on my arms are way too tight. So much it hurts.

"Go back to post," one of the big guys drones.

"Uh, okay," Gary says. "Have a good one."

The iron door slams in Gary's face.

Both of the giants holding me laugh tonelessly and swing me around.

This isn't good. Not at all.

Those black squiggles mean very bad things are going on here.

They march me through hallways until we reach

the numerals 216, stamped into a windowless metal door.

"Take it," one of the orderlies grunts shoving me into the not so loving embrace of the other. "I'll open the door."

"Hurry up," the one holding me says. "It stinks."

I fight my natural instincts to be a smartass and spout something awesome. I'm supposed to be playing a part here. Can't let them know I'm not really nutty.

The door opens to a medium sized room. The floor and walls are all steel, and shiny. In the very center of the room sits a bald man in a gray suit. His legs are crossed and he holds some electronic device in his hands. He looks at me as the orderlies usher me in.

"Ah," says the man. "Welcome." He nods at the orderly not holding me.

From a stack of them, the guy picks up another steel chair and places it in front of the bald dude. I'm shoved into the chair. I keep pretending. Keep twitching and mumbling.

"Thank you, gentlemen," the bald guy says. "Please step out while I have a moment with our new young friend here."

They say nothing and leave the room.

He stares at me for a very long time. I keep up with my act. Even stand up and pace before sitting down again.

Then he says, "I'm Mr. Hannon. It's really good

to finally meet you, Chase."

And like that, my act falters. I blink at him.

Hannon grins. "Come now. Don't be so surprised. I've actually been expecting you. How's that unit treating you? Well, I hope."

"You're… one of them," I manage through the cloud of shock.

"I just have a special talent, I suppose you could say. I see what's really in front of me. Why do you think I gave the order to have you brought straight to me? Usually new arrivals go through evaluations before seeing me. Sometimes I don't even meet our patients."

"Well you're just a bundle of joys, aren't ya?" It just rolls out of my mouth.

Hannon's grin widens. "So you are sarcastic after all. Very good." He taps something on the electronic device.

"Where's my mom?"

He winks. "She's under my care."

"Let her go."

He sighs and levels his eyes on me. His grin disappears. "I'm afraid that's not possible, bud. She's very ill, you know. Needs constant care. Care which only I can provide."

"What the hell are you doing to her? Where is she?"

"You," Hannon says, "will meet her soon enough. For now, let's talk, shall we?"

"Uh, no."

Hannon's eyes grow dim. His mouth turns downward. "No need to be rude. I'm here to help." Something slithers just under his skin. Reminds me of Ti.

"Dude, you're not even human at all."

"Oh? And why do you say that, Chase?"

"Because you got the same shit going on as Ti."

He snorts. "And what do you know of Ti?"

"I know she's dead, how's that?"

Hannon curls his upper lip. Well, well, this is escalating quickly, ain't it? Makes me all warm and fuzzy.

"You... killed her?" His voice is flat. All the scares.

Shake my head. "Nope. Death did. But I watched. Well, a little. I had other places to go, people to see. You know how that works. Busy, busy."

He doesn't say anything. Taps on his device. He takes a few deep breaths and eventually his mood seems to change. He's all calm again.

"All right. Now that it's out, were you also the one who released the chosen?"

I laugh. Can't help it. When it subsides, I say, "Chosen? Really? You mean the *victims*, dipnuts."

"They were chosen to bring true life to all units. The skin of human youth."

"You're an idiot."

He moves the device aside, smiles. "I think it's time you meet your mother."

THE SKIN FACTORY

The door opens behind me.

~ 2 ~

THE MAMMOTH ORDERLIES lift me out of the chair like I'm nothing and swing me around. I face an open doorway.

Behind me, Hannon says, "Aben will arrive soon, but I feel you should at least say hello to your mother. I think she'll like that, don't you?"

My feet never touch the floor as they carry me towards the doorway.

The old guard from outside stops outside the room. His light blue eyes touch on me, then gaze past. "Mr. Hannon. We have a problem."

Hannon's voice is all kinds of craggy when he says, "Oh? And what would that be, Cap? I think if there was a real problem I'd know. And why aren't you at your post?"

"My apologies, sir. But it's the new guy, Mike, he's having a seizure and—"

Hannon rushes by me. He slaps Cap hard across

the face. "That's not my problem, Cap. Not at all. It's yours. You know that. So why are you *here*?"

Cap backs away a little. "Well, I thought since you're a doctor, you might be able to help. Didn't want to call an ambulance if there was no need."

"Get out of here," Hannon growls. "You disgust me."

Cap starts away. Again his eyes touch on me, then return to Hannon. "What do I do with Mike?"

Hannon shakes his head, waves a dismissive hand. "Shoot him. Bury him out back."

"I—what? He's just a kid, Hannon. He just needs some medical—"

Hannon grabs the collar of Cap's jacket and yanks him forward. "Shoot him. Bury him. What parts of that do you not understand? If you don't follow my orders, you'll be right alongside that worthless cow in a shallow grave, got me?"

Cap doesn't look scared at all. Looks like he might actually punch Hannon in the face. Instead, he only nods. Hannon releases him. Cap walks away.

Hannon clears his throat, adjusts his suit a bit and turns to me.

"Now," he says. "Let's go see your mother."

Great, I'm stuck in this building with a creature even more unstable than Aben. Very short fuse. All it'll take is saying the wrong thing at the wrong time and I might cease to exist. Figures. I hope Sara and Andi made it inside. If so, they better get Mom out and forget about me. If Hannon catches them, things could go from bad to downright horrible in a blink.

The orderlies, more like Guards in human skin, let me walk on my own, though keep a tight grip on my arms. Out of the room, they turn me left. Hannon walks ahead, humming some weird tune under his breath. I get this incredible urge to kick him in the ass, but dismiss the impulse.

I'm turned right. We walk a long corridor, turn right again.

This hall, the left side is partially glass. There's a six or seven foot gap leading down into some black pit. And across from this is another hall with a partial glass wall. For a brief second I think I spot the tops of two heads peek over the actual three foot high wall. Girl heads. Then they're gone.

Stay down, I think. *If that's really you two, stay down and wait.*

I'm propelled forward to a T intersection. Here Hannon stops the orderlies. His dark gaze fixes on me. "She is not well," he says. "Understand that before we enter her room. And with you inhabiting a unit, she will not know it's you. But I will allow you to see her one last time before Aben arrives. Least I can do."

"Your kindness is overwhelming. Please. Stop. Sniffle-sniffle."

His lips tighten together, but he turns away and continues on without saying anything. We take a left, then a right. The numbers on the doors read: 1310, 1309, 1308... etc.

Hannon stops at the door marked 1300. He produces a silver keycard from the pocket of his suit pants, swipes it across a small reader. It beeps and a green light blinks above the door knob.

"Okay, Chase, I give you... your mother." He opens the door.

The room is made of all shiny steel like the one I met Hannon in. The only differences are the squat dresser with a small, battery powered lamp fixed on top and a narrow bed that might as well be a cot. Pah. Probs *is* a cot.

But the lamp is the only light source in the room so whatever is beyond the cot is doused in thick shadows.

And dear all the gods ever produced and discarded, what is that *smell*? It's like the old sack of potatoes Mom forgot under the kitchen sink one time. All wet and moldy. This rancid, *blach* stink.

"Mrs. Dunning, dear," Hannon announces. "You have a visitor."

Of course he doesn't say my name. Of course not. What fun would that be? Stupid butt nipple.

A sigh floats on the gross air. The lamp flickers. The entire room seems to tilt to the left a little. I get this weird sense of something bad approaching. Of hateful, predatory eyes watching me.

The orderlies release me. My biceps ache where they had gripped me. I'm absently rubbing the right one when soft shuffling sounds move in my direction.

A figure emerges from the shadows. Stringy, dark hair drapes over its face. Its paper white arms dangle at its sides. Its bare feet look scabbed, more than a few toes missing. But these things only hold my attention for a few seconds. What traps my gaze is the swollen belly protruding out of a long slit in the hospital gown. What holds it are the black veins squiggling all over bleached skin. What keeps it fixed are the bulges that appear to move around as the human-ish figure makes its way closer and closer towards me.

I'm about to ask Hannon where my mom is when my sight picks up something familiar.

Mom went through a wild spurt in her early twenties, Grandma told me once before she passed away. During this "spurt," Mom partied hard, drank a lot of booze, probably did more than a few types of drugs, slept around... and got a tattoo.

The tattoo is a neat conglomeration of a pentagram, a cross, and some Celtic symbol that means peace. Right above her left breast, near the collarbone.

I've seen it hundreds of times, especially during the summer when Mom would wear tank tops or lower cut shirts. I know it well.

And here it is.

I hadn't noticed it before because the hospital gown was covering it. But as she moved so did the gown.

Boom.

"No." My voice is barely above a whisper. More like a rasp.

The creature shuffling closer sighs again. The stink, I realize—that rotten potato reek—emanates from *her*.

"M-*Mom*?"

She stops. Her head tilts to the right, allowing the stringy hair to move away from her face. Ugh, I wish it hadn't. It's her, but an older, uglier version. Half circles hang under her eyes like permanent bruises. Deep lines at the corners of her mouth cut downward, making her look like she's in constant grimace mode. Her face looks... doughy.

"Mom? It's me... Chase."

Her eyes, like shiny chips of onyx, stare blankly at me.

Not good.

"Really," I say. "I'm in a different body, but it's —"

"Deeeaaad," Mom wheezes.

"I know," I say. "My other body died. But this is really me." Oh, wait. "I mean inside this girl body it's *me*."

Her head straightens, stringy hair thankfully covering the doughy face once more. She shuffles forward. Stops. Shuffles. Stops.

"Mom, I—"

"A waste of time, Chase," a deep voice rumbles

through the room. The click-clack of hard soled shoes sound on the steel floor.

From out of the shadows behind Mom, Aben's handsome, grinning face appears. He stops beside Mom, hands clasped in front of him. He blows out a dramatic sigh.

"Ah, here's my little trouble maker at last. I trust my stolen unit has treated you well?"

I try to spout my smartassness all over the situation, but I'm too shocked for words right now.

He chuckles, glances from me to my mom. "Yes. A waste of time. She wouldn't remember you even if you managed to convince her you're her son." He winks. "I saw to that personally."

"What..." I swallow down a lump forming in my throat. "What did you do to her?"

Aben winks again. One of his long fingered hands glides over Mom's huge, swollen belly. "Everything she wanted. I made her a mother again."

My eyes flick from her belly to Aben to her belly, back to Aben.

"You sick motherfu—"

Aben explodes through my words with giant blasts of laughter. Once it dies down, he says, "Not like that, exactly, my dear Chase. Not quite."

Something pushes from inside my mom. Her stomach stretches outward a few inches, retracts. Things move all over inside. Like she's full of... snakes...

"What the shit did you do to her?"

I start towards Aben, ready to say eff it and at least get a good punch in before he turns me to dust.

He holds up a hand and it's like some sort of force field. A couple feet away, I simply bounce backwards.

Godammit.

"I gave her the greatest of gifts, my boy. She's Mother to all now. A mother of purpose."

Hannon giggles somewhere to my left. Okay, if I can't punch Aben, than at least I should beat the living hell out of *that* jerkoff. I turn to do just that when Aben speaks again.

"She is the *source*. No more mining. No more waiting."

Blink. "Okay, I'll bite, what the eff are you talking about?"

Aben lowers his head a bit. His narrow eyes stab into me. Again, his long fingers caress my mother's huge belly. "Guess."

"Get your ugly-ass hands off my mom!"

He chuckles, but doesn't remove his hand. I watch manicured fingers glide back and forth, back and forth. All he's doing is pissing me off more. And it's working.

"What do you mean?" I ask, trying to keep my rage in check. The rage route is definitely the wrong one. Maybe if I play my cards differently…

Aben's fingers glide, stroke, glide. "What do you think I mean, my boy?"

My eyes linger on her stomach. Her horrible, bloated, black-veined stomach. At the bulges that push and slither inside. At Aben's caressing fingers. It only takes a handful of seconds for realization to strike.

"You piece of shit!"

Welllp, that escalated quickly. Toss them subtlety cards out the window, here we go.

Aben says, "Ingenious, really, the human body. So fragile, yet so diverse and flexible."

"Get it out of her," I scream. "Right now or I'll tear your bastard head off."

He laughs. Of course he does. What I just threatened is an impossibility. He is, like it or not, god-ish. He's powerful in strength and magic and... everything. An ancient being that's been hiding in the background of religion since before humans knew what good and evil was. Before God and Satan. Before even the Egyptian gods. This creature is something more. And after millions of years, it's finally ready to stake its claim in the world.

Through my mom.

Impregnating her with the Obsidious.

"Now, now," Aben soothes. "I'm still prepared to offer you a position at my side. There is no more time to think about it. Either yes or no. If yes, you'll be the prince of this world. If no... well, I think you can figure out what'll happen then."

"And my mom? What will happen to her?"

"She will remain Mother to you and all. We will

draw the Obsidious from her womb and, with the help of your sister, implant it throughout the human race. Think about it, Chase. Let your mind dwell on it. A world without war. A world with everyone made equal. No more good, no more evil. Only Obsidious."

Shake my head. "Dude, you're effin' nuttybars. What you're doing *is* evil. You're taking away what being human means! The choices, the reason, the love and compassion. Yeah, sure, we're fruitbatty sometimes, and we obliterate each other, but that's just how it is."

His narrow glare fixes on me again. "Up until this point I've been very kind, Chase. Any other god would have destroyed you. Not I. You've shown me how strong you truly are by persevering. But time grows very short and I need an answer. Will you reign by my side, or will you choose extinguishment?"

I stare at Mom's belly, and for the life of my unit, I have nothing to say.

~ 3 ~

BEEP.

It happens so fast. Like split-second fast.

The old guard from the front gates—Cap—bursts through the doorway, pistol drawn.

A loud blast explodes, instantly deafening me. Then everything slows down. Like we're all submerged in water.

A black hole rips open the chest of the huge orderly to my right. The hand holding me clenches, releases, and the giant body collapses to the floor.

There are no sounds, according to my unit's deafened ears.

Fire flashes from the muzzle of Cap's gun, and the other orderly falls in slow motion. Then I'm free. I duck, move as fast as I can to the far-left wall, though it still feels too slow. Like I'm running in a vat of pudding. I crouch beside a small dresser.

Cap's pistol bursts fire three more times as he

charges into the room. In a blink, Hannon's head disappears from its neck. Another body falls in drunken, dizzy slow motion.

Thick gunsmoke consumes the air. The unit coughs, trying to breathe.

Movement near the door draws my attention away from Cap. A figure, a familiar figure.

I scream, I think. I shout at her to, "Look out!" and "Run!"

But either Andi doesn't hear me, or I'm really not shouting at all. Being deaf, I can't tell. Stupid Cap and his stupid gun-toting bravado.

Then my ears begin to ring. Shrill, long *eeeeee*'s.

Andi and Sara duck through the doorway and stop short at the scene. Both of them are all wide eyes and open mouths.

Out of the swirling smoke, Mom emerges, her distended stomach swaying and jiggling like a big ball of gelatin. I have no idea where Cap and Aben went. Not that I care right now anyway. Mom and her swollen gelatin belly has my full, horrified attention.

Good job, Mom.

Her stringy hair drifts listlessly across a grinning face. Her eyes are black. The cold, dead stare of a great white shark.

Sounds, muffled and weird at first, find my ears. Then, gradually, my hearing clears. Grunts. Thuds. Shouts. Smacks. Something growls.

Mom blinks. And for that second or two, I see

her. I see my mom. Even the eyes are hers. Then, all black. Her distended belly writhes. Like a bag full of venomous snakes.

"Andi, look out!" I shout.

Andi looks around, but apparently she can't see me through the smoke. She can see Mom, though. Except, Mom isn't all Mom anymore. She's carrying the Obsidious and it's no doubt controlling her. She's becoming a mere vessel. Then again, maybe there's nothing left of her now. Maybe it has taken over completely. If so... there's no saving her now.

"Mom?" Andi says, and steps closer to the lurching thing.

Mom tilts her head, very much like she did when I said Mom. Like she's trying to remember us, except, Obsidious.

Grunts and shouts going on behind me.

Cap and Aben struggle. Cap punches Aben hard enough to dislodge his lower jaw. It hangs loosely for a moment, then snaps back into place. How is Cap so strong? No normal human could ever—

Then the old guard glances my way and I see. Oh yes, I see. It's not the face of an old man, but darkness. A very familiar, smoky, white-eyed darkness. The face wavering over the old man's is Bal's.

Aben lifts Bal in the air and growls, "Traitor." Then he throws Bal into the nearest wall.

Bal bounces off, collapses on the floor. Not

moving.

I turn and Andi is literally inches from Mom. Sara looks totally terrified. She looks at me, then at Andi. I can tell she has no clue what to do and I don't blame her. I can't think of anything either. Need to get them all out of this room, but—

"Enough," Aben bellows.

I manage three steps towards Mom and Andi, then...

Darkness.

Through the black, voices. Someone is talking to someone else. Something beeps constantly.

I try to open my eyes, but either they're not working or I'm dreaming. Or the unit simply refuses to open them. Her terror is totally maxed out. Poor thing.

Yet, as I listen to the voices I realize I'm not dreaming. And the black is receding. First gray, then blurry colors. I'm on the floor. The cold, steel floor.

"All it takes is one spore, and the Obsidious multiplies to thousands within seconds."

That's Aben. I'd recognize the smugness anywhere.

"You son of a bitch."

And that's Andi.

"Aben, you know full well that this is not the way."

Who the eff is *that*? Then I get it. Bal.

Aben chuckles. "Ah, and what do you know, traitor? Absolutely nothing."

My vision clears to the unit's normal levels, but my view is of someone's shiny dress shoes. Or the backs of them, anyway. I watch them step this way and that. Listening to the constant beep, beep, beep of what I now recognize as an IV machine thing.

Something metal clinks.

"Once you're injected, you'll see what I mean," Aben says. "You'll understand the importance and how humanity will be saved."

"Like my brother would say, you must've ate a lot of paint chips as kid," Andi spouts and I almost laugh out loud. Total proud bro moment.

A woman moans. Mom?

Then, as if to confirm my thought, "Mom? Mom, it's me. It's Andi. I love you."

Aben laughs. "She doesn't—"

"A-Andi?" Mom's voice is crackly, but it's definitely hers.

"Yes!" Andi cries. "It's really me! Mom, listen, you have to push it out of you. You can't let them win. You—"

A sharp crack sounds. Did Aben just slap Andi? Shit, I think so.

"Idiot girl," Aben growls. "She's mine now. She belongs to Obsidious!"

"She's my *mom*," Andi growls back. "And you hit like a baby guppy, by the way."

"Wh-where am I?" Mom crackles. "Who—

what's going on?"

"Shh, now," Aben whispers. "Shut your eyes and sleep."

"Mom! Don't let them win! Fight them!" Andi's voice squeaks on the last word.

I have to stop this. Somehow. And where the hell is Sara?

I'm on my right side, staring at the backs of Aben's shiny shoes. Can't see anything else. I don't even hear Sara. Which isn't good.

There's another metallic clink.

Quietly, I get up. Bal's gaze shifts the tiniest bit towards me, returns to Aben, the creature which I stand behind now. Andi and Bal are tied to a couple of beds. So far, Andi doesn't see me. This works. She'll give it all away.

Mom is strapped to a table, hooked up to some weird machine that might be an IV's evil cousin. The tube going into Mom's wrist is black. The fluid in the bag hooked above the machine, black. Everything... black.

Aben has a large syringe in his hand when he says, "Time to enlighten you both."

"Aben," Bal says in an old man's voice. "We have worked together for centuries. Listen to me, this is not the way."

I glance at Bal as Andi says, "What are you talking about? I thought you were on our side!"

"I have no side, Andi."

Glare at Bal and silently hope he falls down a

well for telling her that.

"Enough," Aben says. And before I know what's happening, he stabs the needle into Mom's huge belly.

She cries out. Her back arches. Her eyes squeeze shut.

I glance around, trying to find something to beat the evil bastard with, and spot Sara instead near the dresser. She hasn't woken up from whatever blackout spell Aben cast. At least that's what I hope. I hope she's just still asleep. She looks so peaceful, even with her fierce reptilian mods. I love her.

Aben pulls the plunger up and the syringe fills with brackish liquid. Like muddy water.

"The Obsidious," Aben says, "was a part of this world long before humans ever formed. It's even older than me."

"Congratulations," Andi says, totally channeling me right now. Another proud bro moment. "If only I had a cookie to give ya."

Aben ignores her. "It has so much knowledge of this earth. Makes sense to let it rule, don't you say?"

"When Obsidious last ruled Earth," Bal says, "it ate all the good out of every living thing it inhabited. Then the Ice Age came and—"

"Spare me your history lessons," Aben growls. "I know what happened."

"Then you know it will inhabit and kill you too."

"Not if I inject it directly. And they have assured me they will not kill their inhabitants."

Bal snorts. "*They* assured you, did they? Interesting."

Aben nods, extracts the needle from Mom's belly. "Soon you'll have all the answers."

He rounds the table Mom is on, syringe raised. His dark gaze stabs into Andi. I guess she's to be the first to try Aben's new Blackout drug. AKA, Obsidious.

Andi tries to wriggle out of the cords holding her wrists to the bed, but they're too tight. So tight the poor girl's fingers are turning purple.

Aben pulls her right pant leg up. Her legs are also tied to the bed, of course. He lowers the syringe. The tip of the needle dimples skin. Another tiny push and it'll be Obsidious Land for Andi—

Out of nowhere, Sara rams into Aben's left side, hard enough to knock him away from Andi's leg. A fist connects with his face. But that's as far as the fight goes. Aben has Sara in his clutches before she can land another punch.

"Idiot girl," Aben says, wrapping a long-fingered hand around her throat. He lifts her into the air.

"Let her go you asshat!" I rip the black tube out of Mom's wrist, fling it over Aben's head and pull it taut against the creature's throat. Pretty much trying to strangle him, as he strangles Sara.

The syringe drops onto Mom's heaving chest.

"A-Andi?" Mom manages between gasps.

But either Andi doesn't hear her or is too concentrated on watching the struggle between

Aben, Sara, and me.

Then I see Andi buck and thrash and heave against the cords holding her. After a few seconds of this, though, she stops. I see glimpses of blood slicking her wrists where the cords are.

Aben drops Sara. She rolls away, coughing and gagging.

"Ah, Chase... I was wondering when you'd wake up. How's my future Scout faring?"

He reaches behind him and flips me over the table, over Andi's bed. I land hard on top of Bal. We blink at each other a moment then I clamber off. I help Sara to her feet.

Aben chuckles deep in his throat.

Then something amazing happens. Andi's left hand slips out of the cord holding it. Her lips are clamped together in obvious pain, wrists shallowly cut by the cord. Just enough to draw blood. The blood... that's what did it. It's like a lubricant. That's how she slipped out. I avert my eyes so Aben doesn't follow my gaze.

I look at Bal. "Why haven't you busted those cords yet?"

He sighs. "I'm waiting."

"For what?"

"You'll see."

"You have no idea, do you?"

"Shut up, Chase."

"You two are being very naughty," Aben says to me and Sara. "I wonder... what your punishments shall be?"

I glance at Bal. He gives me a firm nod. Whatever *that* means. Maybe approval? Pssh, I doubt it. More like a do-all-the-work-while-I-lay-here-doing-nothing nod.

Aben grins, rounds the table and moves towards us as we press our backs against the wall. We can't fight him. He's too strong. I try to ignore the slow movements coming from Andi's bed.

For the time being, she doesn't exist for Aben. Definitely a good thing.

My sight drifts over Andi (eyes never pause on her) as Mom's eyes open, shut, open. They're hers. I think. For now at least. Tears glitter in them. Her chest works with every gasping breath. I cup her sweaty cheek in my hand and mouth the words, "I love you Mom." The corners of her mouth quirk. Her eyes brighten (with recognition?) a smidge.

In a withered, trembling hand, she holds Aben's huge syringe. I look from it to her. She nods the tiniest bit. Then Andi stands on the other side of the bed. So quiet to get free and slip out of bed. I forgot how ninja she can be! Mom looks at her, smiles. Andi takes the syringe from Mom's trembling hand. Then my sister disappears behind Aben.

~ 4 ~

THE ANCIENT BEING BENDS so that their eyes meet mine. "You can't stop this, Chase. There is nothing left for you but an eternity of pain."

From the corner of my eye, I catch the subtlest of movement. Bal?

"Guess that other option was thrown down the pooper, eh?" I wink at Aben.

"In a matter of speaking," Aben says. "There never really was an option for you."

Bal steps around the cot, then… falls. Just drops like a big sack of oranges.

The sound is enough to make Aben glance in that direction. "That you, Bal? Don't worry, your time is coming—"

A jet black shadow materializes beside me and shoves Aben backwards with so much force he actually flies a few feet into the air. Thankfully, Andi moved aside enough to not get plowed over. Aben lands flat on his back. Hard.

"Whoa," I say. "Bal, that was—"

"Get out of here you fool," Bal growls and swirls his being towards Aben. Like smoke, Bal is constantly moving and shifting.

Sara tugs on to get me moving. She points at the door. Andi is already helping our mom to sit. Aben is already on his feet. He's grinning. Always grinning.

"Grew some balls over the last century I see," Aben says. "Was wondering when you'd show your true self. Your son would be proud!"

"Shut up," Bal spits. All the growls. "You have no right to speak of my son. I should have never agreed to work for you."

Aben chuckles and swipes a hand through the air. A purplish light flashes and Bal stumbles back a few steps.

"Too bad you'll never join him in your After," Aben says.

Bal whooshes forward, winds his smoky self around Aben, solidifies behind the old monster. Aben's grin never droops.

"Old tricks," Aben whispers, and turns.

Sara is trying to lead me around the monsters towards the door. Then I notice Andi.

"What obsesses him so, will also destroy him," Mom whispers. She's sitting up, but still on the table.

I frown at her. She glances at her belly. Tears

patter onto the black, pulsing veins. Her gaze shifts to the syringe in Andi's hand.

"What do you mean?" I move closer to her as Andi moves towards Aben and Bal.

"I love you... Chase. I l-love Andi. Tell her. Please... tell her for me."

"Tell her yourself. We're gettin' outta here."

But she places a hand on my chest and pushes me away. Her head shakes slowly. "Can't let him win." Her voice is getting all raspy again. "Can't... it hurts... they're... eating me. They're..."

I watch her eyes change from blue to black, like small globes filling with ink. Saliva drools out of her mouth. The hand on my chest turns into a claw, fingernails digging in.

I pull away. She cackles in a low, dark voice and lies back down on the table.

Sara tugs on me to go, and Andi is almost to the dueling creatures, syringe raised.

I tell the unit: Be Strong

I tell her: Let's Save The World

Then I snatch the syringe from Andi and sprint at Aben

"Chase," Andi screams, but it's too late to stop. Too late to chicken out. Too late...

Aben is in mid-turn when I slam the needle deep into the middle of his back. I don't know how much Obsidious I inject before I'm knocked off our feet. Agony explodes through the me and the unit. Something Aben threw? Shot at us?

"*No*," Andi cries and then she's at my side. She's crying, stroking the side of my face as she whispers, "I lost you once. Not again."

Aben is bent over, shuddering, the syringe still stuck in his back.

I'm not dying, but maybe I look like it? I mean, *ow*, this shit hurts, but I think I'll live. I get it, though. If Mom can't be saved, I'm all Andi has left.

Bal and his smokiness materializes over us. Aben makes thick grunting noises.

"Chase, are you okay?" Bal swirls, solidifies.

"Yeah," I manage through gritting teeth. "Just hurt."

"Get up and get out of here, he's—"

Aben's fist explodes out of Bal's chest. Bits of black goo spray in every direction. Bal rears. A sick gurgling sound fills my ears. Aben yanks his arm out, stumbles towards Mom. He appears to be choking on something.

The syringe I stabbed him with is still in his back. Still buried deep. But there's still some Obsidious inside the tube. Not all of it was injected before he hit me with, well, whatever the shit he hit me with.

My sight moves from Aben to my mom, to Sara, to Andi. Around and around. Searing heat spreads through my chest. Every muscle tenses. If this is what true rage feels like I'd say I have a serious case of it.

I scream. No words. Just this loud, horrible scream of anger. All my hurt and sorrow and rage. All exploding out of me.

Aben is bent over Mom doing something. Doesn't even flinch when I scream. Doesn't move when Sara shouts my name from the door.

I stand and burst forward, propelled by hate. Surging with anger. Seething with sorrow.

Blink and I'm pushing the syringe plunger. I'm injecting all of whatever is in the syringe into Aben's back. He howls, swipes at me with his long fingered hands. Somehow I manage to dodge the lethal things and step away.

Aben spins and holy poopweasels! His face... it's all... fat. Swollen. Gone are the handsome, chiseled looks. His skin is a deep shade of purple streaked with black veins. His throat, also swollen massively, visibly pulses. Black goop spurts from his howling mouth.

"*Chase, Andi,*" Sara yells. "Come on!"

She breaks the hold Aben's gruesome visage has on me. I shoot her a look. "I'm not leaving Mom!"

For a wonder, she doesn't protest. Instead she runs to where Andi stands between the door and me.

I start towards the table where Mom is. Where Aben sort of flounders on her, clawing gouges through his white suit. A white suit now turning black from all the goop coming out of him.

I'm barely three feet away when Mom sits up.

Her arms clamp around Aben's chest. Our eyes meet.

"I love you," she rasps.

Then she sinks her teeth into the side of Aben's neck.

The black goop becomes a fount of gross. It shoots to the ceiling, splashes everywhere. Somehow I manage not to get slathered with any of it. Aben's arms stretch out like the horizontal beam of a cross.

In a single fluid motion, Mom rips out a chunk of Aben's throat.

Aben squeals. His entire body jitters. He begins to slump. A smoky substance billows out of the open throat wound.

Mom spits the chunk of Aben out and falls back onto the bed. Her legs shake. They're all I can really see of her with Aben thrashing around.

Sara is pulling a wide-eyed Andi towards the door.

If Bal survived, he's not here anymore. Not a trace.

I shove Aben aside. He falls to the floor, gagging and choking and spurting all that yucky black everywhere.

The table Mom is on has wheels. I unlock them, careful not to touch any of the black stuff Aben is getting all over the place. I have a feeling touching it would be very bad for me. I push Mom towards the door, and that's when her swollen belly bursts.

Something black crawls out of what used to be

her stomach. Something with a large maw full of teeth and claw-like tentacles.

Andi sits down hard on the floor, hands raking through her hair, screaming. Her eyes are huge, caught in sheer horror. But... Mom...

Mom's head lolls from side to side as the thing jostles around. Other than that, she doesn't move. That's what really freezes me in place. There's no doubt in my mind. Mom is dead.

Soft, barely there, Aben's voice, "No..."

He's propped up against Bal's cot. Black stuff covers pretty much every inch of him. His skin is droopy. His hair... gone. His teeth are tiny, pointy spears in his working mouth. He's dying, I realize.

I run to Andi before Sara breaks out of her horrified gaze.

The thing lashes its clawed tentacles at me. It misses with all five. Barely. A talon slices through the sleeve of my shirt, though thankfully doesn't touch the skin. I slide to Andi, grab her arms, and yank her to her feet. She's still screaming, eyes locked on the monster writhing in the crater of Mom's stomach.

So I slap her. Hard.

Her head rocks back. Her scream cuts off and she glares at me. Like full on I'm-going-to-rip-you-apart glare.

"Easy," I shout over the howling monstrosity. "We have to go!"

She looks at the thing again. I step in between

and shake my head. "Mom is gone. We have to go!"

Andi shakes her head. "Nononono."

Shit. Okay...

I drag her away, making sure we give the creature a wide berth. Are those tentacles growing? Holy baboon nipples, I think they are!

They stretch towards us, claws grasping and snapping. It howls. Not like a single howl, but like millions all at once.

We're almost to Sara when Bal appears in front of us. He's taller than I remember. Scarier. His white eyes narrow on me.

"Well, it's about time you do *something*," I say. "Even if it's just standing there looking all sinister and shit."

Bal sighs, nods at the thing lashing from Mom's ruined stomach. "I'll get rid of it."

I glance back, then at Bal. "How? Isn't that like the ultimate Obsidious right there?"

His eyes soften. "There are other places than this, as you know."

"Yeah. But what about Aben?"

"He's finished," Bal says. "All of his essence is draining out. Won't be long for him now."

"I thought he was like... eternal?"

Bal shakes his head. "Nothing but two beings are eternal, Chase. You know that, even if you refuse to acknowledge the fact. Now get out of here and live your life."

He moves aside. We start towards the door, but I

stop. When I look back, Bal shows me his smile for the first time. It's hideous, but genuine.

"It was a pleasure knowing you, Chase Dunning. I may call upon you again, someday."

I smile back. "You better not, you crazy bastard, but… likewise."

Bal grunts, turns and leaps onto the writhing Obsidious thing. It lets loose the loudest shriek when Bal shoves his fist into its middle. Then all of its tentacles wrap around him like thick, black snakes. The claws clamp into his smoky skin. He cries out in obvious agony.

"*Bal*," I shout.

I make it about three or four steps, then Bal and the Obsidious vanish.

All that remains are a few tendrils of black smoke. Even my mom is gone. The table where she was drips black goop for a few seconds, and then that too disappears. In fact, all of the mayhem that occurred in this room, all the evidence, fades away before my eyes. Poof. Bub-bye now. Later, tater.

The only thing here is Aben.

A slumped, dark figure across the room. He doesn't move. At all. The black blood that is his essence has stopped spurting and oozing. It all spreads around him in this giant, dark pool.

I feel a tugging on my arm.

Sara.

"Come on, baby," she says in a voice somewhere between weariness and shock. "Let's go."

Andi stares at the table where Mom had lain. She absently wipes a tear from her cheek and faces me. "Do you think she went to Heaven?"

There's no right or wrong answer to this so I say, "Yes."

She sniffles. "Is it… over now?"

I smile and take her in my arms. Her entire body seems to melt into me. "Yes," I whisper to her forehead. "*So* over."

Sara and Andi step out of the room, but something, a weird buzz, stops me. I turn.

Aben and his massive pool of blackness is gone.

Poof.

Bub-Bye.

HOPE

~ 1 ~

WE'RE NOT DOING MUCH planting in our garden, Sara and I. Unless you call rolling around in the dirt and laughing like goobs planting.

The morning sunshine is warm, like kisses from a loving god, some might say. Soon, summer will be over and we'll have to batten down everything for the winter. Northern winters, I hear, are nasty things.

Sara shoves me onto my back, straddles me and proceeds to shove seed potatoes down my shirt. Her scaly green skin shimmers in the sun. So beautiful. We're still in our units, but less and less we think of it that way. Less and less we feel like separate things. We are melding to the units, which I've come to accept and love.

It's been, what, three, four months since all the craziness? Kind of lost any sense of time since building the cottage. We're still getting accustomed to living out in the wilderness, but so far I think we're doing okay.

If not for the money in the backpack Bal left to me, none of this would be happening right now. I had to buy all the logs to build the cabin. I mean, I could've totally went lumberjack and did it all on my own, but this way just made more sense. Less time consuming.

After it was all over, we went back to Andi's former shop, or whatever it had really been. Aben's spell on it had lifted. It was just an old, abandoned machine shop again. Squat and gray. Empty.

The inside was covered in dust... well, except for the chair. I recognized it immediately. The tattoo chair remained exactly where it had been. No dust covered it. But... resting in the seat was the backpack.

Over a million dollars rolled into tight wads filled it. Bal must've placed it there at some point.

Finally, Sara and I do what we came out here to do, planting the potatoes. We're still laughing, though. These days it's all the smiles and laughs.

Andi spends a lot of time inside the cabin, but not because she's depressed or anything. She's gotten into studying other religions and cultures, especially the spiritual aspects of each. At night, before we all head to bed, she'll go on and on about how every religion is the same, only different. Like they all share this same underlying belief of greater goods and vile evils. That's one of the things anyway. Painting is her other thing. She'd paint day and night every day if I let her. Landscapes. Rotten, bug filled logs. A close-up of a dandelion. Pretty much anything she sees in her head or outside of it. And she's getting damn good, too.

Dig a shallow hole, toss a seed potato in, cover it up. On to the next hole, the next potato. Reminds me of the shitty ol'days installing teeth in the Factory, only... this is fun. This is for us. This is a *good* thing.

Later, I'm trying to chop down this small tree for firewood when—in mid-swing—a voice says, "How are you, foolish boy?"

I miss the tree with the axe head and whack the handle into the trunk instead. Pain rattles through my hands and up my arms. The axe thumps to the ground.

"Hoppin' jiggly poofs," I shout and spin around. "Bal, what the hell?"

And there he is. Smoky black. Unblinking white eyes. "My apologies."

I grunt, pick up the axe and say, "A little warning next time, huh? What's up?"

Bal nods. "Always the smartass. Not even a thank you for everything I've given you."

He's right. I do owe him a lot. Or at least a thank you, so...

"Thanks, man. Really. Without the money we wouldn't have this place."

Bal nods again. "Of course, but a thank you is

not why I've come here."

I lean on the axe handle, lift an eyebrow. "Okay… ?"

"I have a proposition for you."

Frown. "Oh? I thought this was it? We all live happily ever after, and stuff."

"Yes," Bal says. "But I've come to offer you a position of great importance."

"Ah." I stroke my chin, all faux sophisticated like. "Of great importance, you say?"

"Stop it. "

Shrug. "Dude, you're being vague."

"I want you to help me build a legion."

"A… legion? Like an army?"

Bal's eyes narrow on me. "Not an army. More like elite assassins. I want you to help me get my son back. I want you to go in and find him so we can rescue him."

"Whoa," I say, holding up my hands. "*Assassins*? For what? Dude, your son is in his destined After. Happy. Isn't that more important than—"

"He is not happy."

"You mean *you're* not happy."

"He is a prisoner," Bal roars. "His After is false!"

"How do you know, though?"

"I did not come here for you to question me. I came to ask you to help me rescue my son."

All around us birds are singing, squirrels are scampering, and this creature is asking me to do the impossible.

"I can't leave Sara and Andi."

"They will be taken care of and——"

"No," I burst out. "I'm over it! All of that otherworldly bullshit! Done! I just wanna live my *life*, man!"

Bal straightens, white glare burning into me. "Is that your answer, Chase?"

"If I have a choice."

The creature says, "You always have a choice."

No brainer. "Then I choose to stay here. You're welcome to come chill whenever, but this thing you're asking of me... dude, I just can't."

Those white eyes are nothing but paper-thin slits cut in a black storm. "So be it."

"Bal, listen, I——"

"There will come a time, foolish boy, when you may regret the choice you made today."

"Is that a threat?"

Black tendrils swirl in a chaotic mess, then Bal is gone, leaving a smoky mist behind.

"Shit," I whisper to the birds and squirrels, and the dissipating smoke in front of me.

~ 2 ~

WE ALL SIT IN THE SMALL living room of the cabin, not talking much, as the fire crackles away in the fireplace.

Sara snuggles in close and I gently stroke her black hair. She's about asleep.

Andi sits in the recliner all the way across the room, reading a book about the Muslim faith, beliefs, and folklore.

It's been a long, but productive day. Physically for Sara and I, mind-wise for Andi. She's soaking everything she can in. Learning about other cultures and religions, and their monsters. I smile at her, but she's too absorbed to notice. Which is cool.

My eyes drift to the fire. All of those flickering oranges, yellows, reds and blues. They capture me, totally entranced.

I just hope we can make it work here. I hope we are allowed to live. Truly live. Grow up. Make memories. Go on fun adventures. Just, live.

And I hope the shadows remain shadows and the darkness remains still.

I hope.

ABOUT THE AUTHOR

Lucas Pederson is the author of ten novels, including CLINT CLUSTERFUK. You can find his books on Amazon. He lives in a small Iowa town with his family... and let's not ask what he keeps in the basement.